Shadows 6

Shadows 6

Edited by
CHARLES L. GRANT

DOUBLEDAY & COMPANY, INC.

GARDEN CITY, NEW YORK

1983

*All of the characters in this book
are fictitious, and any resemblance
to actual persons, living or dead,
is purely coincidental.*

Library of Congress Cataloging in Publication Data
Main entry under title:
Shadows 6.
1. Horror tales, American. I. Grant, Charles L.
II. Title: Shadows six.
PS648.H6S535   1983   813'.0872'08
ISBN 0-385-18259-7

Library of Congress Catalog Card Number 82–45527

Contents

Introduction

There are Critters, and then there are critters.

In Dark Fantasy (as in science fiction) there have been considerably more of the former than the latter until recently. In films, novels, and short fiction the Creature from the Black Lagoon, the "It" that came from outer space, and the ugly in the cellar that may or may not be a long-lost uncle dominated because producers and publishers were under the mistaken impression that the viewing audience and readers were eager to face directly whatever fears these Critters symbolized, or were direct manifestations of.

And it worked for a while, because the Frankenstein monster and Dracula and the Wolfman were unusual enough in a nonvisually oriented society to produce the screams and shivers necessary for success.

Unfortunately, the movie theaters proliferated and the films had to compete and by the time television came along we were stuck with the hideous sun demon and the crab monsters and Abbott and Costello meeting Jekyll and Hyde. Television (and now VCRs) multiplied exposure a thousandfold, and it's only with fondness rather than a chill that many of us now see Karloff twitching his hand on Colin Clive's laboratory table.

They don't much work anymore, these Critters, and that's amply proved by the botch John Carpenter made of John Campbell's "Who Goes There?" The director's heart was in the right place, but he should have remembered (perhaps even re-viewed) *Halloween* or *The Fog* to see what had made it all work the first time. It certainly wasn't watching a husky turn itself inside out.

But then, on the bright side, there are critters.

They don't look like Critters because they're generally ordinary people, or they're suggestions of ordinary people—like movement in a fog, or shadows on an empty street, or voices not quite recognizable on the other side of a bedroom door. Or, as in *'Salem's Lot* or *Shadowland* or *The Moorstone Sickness*, they're *exactly* like you and me until you turn your back on them, and then they're not like you at all.

And that is perhaps the single greatest fear that any of us ever have—that what we know to be true, that what we know is so and will not change because it has never changed before, isn't true anymore, isn't so, and everything can change, not always for the better.

Dark Fantasy does not illuminate the dark side of life, as we don't want to know it; it merely casts a little light in that direction, just enough light to create outlines, and hints, and naturally, the shadows. And from that we can learn much more than we can in full daylight. In daylight nothing hides or is hidden; at dusk, there is just enough light, and just enough dark, to make us lock the doors.

It's sad to see the Critters go, but it's much more fun to deal with critters.

Charles L. Grant
Newton, New Jersey 1982

Shadows 6

Suppose you wake up one morning, look in the bathroom mirror, and see a stranger looking back at you. Unsettling, but nothing you haven't encountered before after an all-night binge. But suppose you wake up one morning, look in the bathroom mirror, and see yourself looking back at you—and you know that suddenly what you're seeing is a critter. Do you shake it off, cut your throat, or do you adapt?

Lori Allen's gentle stories have appeared frequently in The Magazine of Fantasy and Science Fiction, *but this, her first appearance in* Shadows, *is wonderfully not typical of her at all.*

WE SHARE

by Lori Allen

People are always telling me how lucky I am. Don't I have a lovely home, a husband who is a good provider, a son who is not a delinquent? What more could a woman want?

Well, for one thing, I hate being alone, I tell them.

Who doesn't? they answer. So what else is new?

And they're right. I should be used to being alone by now. When I was a kid I was sick so often I never got around to making many friends. My father was fighting in Germany. My mother was working a double shift.

Mom did share with me though. There were these two spooky programs on radio, *Suspense* and *Inner Sanctum.* Mom used to love them. Only she was too easily frightened to listen alone.

I didn't complain. Like any normal kid, I grabbed at any chance to stay up late. To be scared stiff. To have nightmares.

Eventually the war ended, we got a television, and my mother got into soap operas. Those I couldn't handle. Demons, ghosts, and things that go bump in the night were one thing, but people talking about getting divorced—that was *really* scary.

And so I was alone again.

Until those first few years when Kevin and I were just married.

And then those first few years when our son, Jeff, was young enough to need me.

It was when Jeff was still growing up that I began to return to "those creaking doors" of childhood radio. Except it wasn't radio anymore. It wasn't television either—television wasn't scary enough for *my* son. Only movies would do. Trouble was, the good ones were all rated R, and Jeff was only fourteen. Would I go with him? Please? If he promised to clean his room, empty the garbage, and be polite to his father for an entire week?

What mother could refuse?

I went, fully prepared to be shocked. At the first sign of violence, I was going to turn my eyes from the screen and direct them downward so I could count the pieces of popcorn spilled on the dark gray floor.

But I didn't look down.

Even at the end, where the girl made the villain literally explode and the screen couldn't look bloodier because there was no spot that was not some shade of red, I didn't look down. It seemed a dance, an arabesque. That there were shreds of flesh in the arabesque seemed inconsequential.

I was hooked.

Unfortunately, when Jeff turned seventeen he wouldn't be caught dead going to the movies with his mother. And when Jeff turned eighteen he went away to college.

Now, since I won't go to the movies alone, the question's closed completely. But I haven't given up my interest. The only difference is, instead of watching the monsters, I read about them.

I'm actually becoming something of an expert. The way I see it, there are three basic kinds of classic monster—Frankenstein's creation, Dracula, and werewolves. The first two were easy enough to study. I had a little more trouble with werewolves.

The only classic I've been able to find isn't even a novel. It passes for a scientific study. The man who wrote the book, Sabine Baring-Gould, didn't even believe in werewolves. In his view, anyone who thought he was a werewolf was the Victorian equivalent of some kind of nut. Which didn't stop Baring-Gould from going into loving gory detail about who ate who and why.

"Careful none of that stuff rubs off on you," Kevin warned me the first and only time he noticed what I was reading.

Don't let me give the wrong impression about Kevin. We have a good marriage, better than most, and I'm sure he loves me, as I love him. Only sometimes when people have been together as long as we have, they can be in the same room and still be in two different houses. Maybe if we argued there'd be some exchange —arguing is sharing, in a way. But we never argue.

Today's our anniversary. We had planned to go out to dinner, but the weather's awful. There's really no choice but to celebrate at home.

As I take the steaks out of the refrigerator, for some reason I find myself looking at them. It is the first time I have ever really looked at chunks of meat. At chunks of flesh. Like werewolves eat.

Never did perfectly innocent porterhouses look so gruesome.

And Kevin insists on them being cooked rare—blue rare—the kind of rare that gives the most blood.

And when I was a kid the blood was saved as a special treat for the youngest, or for the one who was just getting over a sickness. I remember it tasting salty-sweet. The fat would cling to my lips for hours.

I wonder if I could talk Kevin into a tuna casserole.

Win some, lose some. Kevin came home late, and he didn't want either a tuna casserole or the steak; he had already eaten. He hated to do this to me seeing as it was our anniversary, but after all, we were adults, weren't we? It had been one of those days. Surely I could understand if all he wanted was a drink and bed? We'd celebrate some other time. Maybe this weekend? Next weekend for sure.

Sure I understood. I wasn't a child who needed instant gratification. I could postpone my pleasures. I was perfectly content to open a can of soup and have a drink myself.

And another drink.

And another.

By the time I got to bed, some two hours after Kevin, I wasn't even feeling sorry for myself anymore.

Usually I don't drink just before I go to bed because it gives me nightmares. Not that I don't have nightmares other times, but the liquor-induced ones have no climax and no ending—they just go on and on from one terror to another and I can't wake up, no matter how hard I try.

And that's exactly the kind of dream I just had.

It was all about me being invaded. Not invaded as in creepy crawly things from outer space. Invaded as in something was growing inside me. Not a baby, or even a cancer. Some kind of unimaginable abortion. Ugly. With teeth. Every time it found a space—between the joints of my fingers, between my teeth and my gums, between the very walls of my heart—it filled it. Filled me. Until I was no longer me.

I just woke up screaming. Except no sound was coming out of my mouth. That's the worst kind of nightmare—when you're screaming for help at the top of your lungs but no one can possibly hear you since you're really not screaming at all.

My mouth is dry. Too much scotch, I guess. I get up and go to the bathroom for a glass of water. I do not turn on the light. Yet in the dark bathroom my jar of cold cream positively sparkles.

It is not only my mouth that is thirsty. I am parched all over. The thermostat is set too high, perhaps, or I may be getting a fever. Or it may be something else. In any case, my skin crackles as I imagine a snake's might, just before it sheds.

I dip my hand in the cold cream. I apply it to my face. It feels blissfully cool, like opening the refrigerator on a summer's day. I smooth it to my neck. My skin drinks deeply.

I take off my nightgown and begin spreading the balm downward. I have never done this before, yet I am not surprised when the oblong of cream over my heart forms ice crystals before it is absorbed. I spread it over my hips and into my navel. I massage it into my pubic hair. I reach behind and, stretching, do my back. I do my thighs and legs and toes, reaching into hidden places.

I hold up my hand, the hand that has smoothed the cream over my body. The palm is broad and the fingers are short, like a werewolf's hands. All werewolves, however, have hair growing out of their palms, and I certainly have none there. But then it could be because my pelt's on inside out. I smile to myself. Then there'd be no sign at all.

I go back to the bedroom. Through the open curtains I see the storm is over. The sky has been transformed from a blurry gray to a clear black. The full moon nearly eclipses the stars.

Kevin is lying on his side of the room, on his twin bed, with his face to the wall. He half wakes when I approach. He tells me he does not want sex tonight.

Nor do I.

I climb on his bed and straddle him. It is almost like making love, especially since I am naked, but the blankets and his pajamas are between us. He feels so far away from me, as if the blankets had always been there, separating us, as if we had never been able to touch, except clumsily, through cloth. So many years together, yet we never really shared.

I have always loved him very much. I have never loved him more than at this moment. Only he is so far away, so impossibly other. Other. Not part of me.

He protests a bit but does not really struggle when I put my mouth upon his throat. I have not kissed him here since we were courting. Like then, he smells of talcum powder. He tastes of salt.

I wish my teeth were sharper. If my teeth were sharper it would be over sooner and not as painful to him. I do not like to see him in pain, so I work as quickly as I can.

I almost have to laugh at my love's attempts at fighting back. I have him pinned down so securely he cannot move. Who would have thought I could be so strong?

He is screaming. I do not like to hear him scream, so I bite a little deeper. The scream stops.

Chest skin is thicker than neck skin, I notice. The hair is longer too, too long to swallow. I spit it out, appalled at the waste.

With each bite I grow closer to Kevin, and closer. Until I feel so full of him that he is part of me. He will always be part of me.

The bedroom is an arabesque of blood. There are shreds of flesh in the arabesque, giving texture to the dance.

Satiated, I kiss the ruin that was my husband. I kiss him full on the mouth, as is a wife's prerogative. He does not respond, but we have been married a long time, and I no longer take that personally.

Reluctantly, I leave him.

I pick up the phone and dial the emergency number.

I tell them it must have been an intruder. Or it could have been a whole gang of intruders. Or maybe it was animals, I don't know. I was asleep, I didn't hear a thing. Perhaps I took some

pills, I don't remember, I know I had too much to drink. Hurry—
he looks so bad!

I take a quick shower. I put on my nightgown. They will expect
tears. I begin to cry.

In the past two days I must have answered the same questions
at least a hundred times— Just who could these intruders have
been? Are you sure you didn't hear anything? Couldn't you at
least have screamed for help?

I'm reasonably sure they believe me.

Then why do I feel so depressed? So alone?

Why is it that even though Kevin's part of me, there's still
something missing? Something I once had, and lost. I do not like
to lose things.

But wait a minute. Maybe it's not all over after all.

Jeff will be home for the funeral. He'll sleep in his old bed,
quiet as you please.

I think it's always nice for a mother and child to share.

Leslie A. Horvitz, whose latest novel is a medical thriller entitled The Donors, *appears in this series for the first time—with a story about a man who, in fact, exists in New York City, though not necessarily in the form you're about to meet him.*

THE APPEARANCES OF GEORGIO

by Leslie A. Horvitz

Let me tell you about Georgio. When he walks it is with a shuffling gait as if he is embarrassed to have intruded on the space his feet must cross. In a few years' time he may well become a hunchback as his bone structure begins to preserve his stooped shoulders and his arched spine. He is short and stubby like a cigar popped butt-end up in an ashtray. When he looks at you it is with dark sorrowing eyes that seem close to tears; his lips are parted all the time as though he is about to speak, to declare his innocence and his solitude. His face is in shadows; he is shaven but still a beard darkens his cheeks and jowls.

Let me tell you about Georgio. He is always alone, always. And he is never without his dark clothes; from a distance he resembles an ancient Greek woman in mourning, or an ancient Spanish one.

One thing is certain: Georgio is never far away. He is always in search, perpetually looking until his eyes glaze over. And what is he looking for? A friend. A woman if he could find one, of course. True enough, true insofar as it goes. But there is more. What he is looking for, who he is looking for, that is something else again. Who he is looking for is me.

No matter that I live downtown and that he lives elsewhere, he invariably locates me. I never notice him at first. He comes in on tiptoe, quietly sidling up to me. He begins to talk, softly in a thick, nearly incomprehensible accent. He will continue like this until I turn and regard him, acknowledging his presence.

He smiles. "We have not seen each other in such a long time," he says. "What do you have to tell me?"

"Nothing," I reply petulantly. "Nothing has happened. There is nothing, absolutely nothing, to tell you."

He looks vaguely disappointed, offended. Then he smiles again and begins as he has in the past, reciting a life story which I heard months ago when first we met at a bar like this one. He tells me he is Italian, living in the United States for two years now. He resides in Brooklyn, he says; he has held twenty jobs in the time he's been here, he says.

"Twenty? Twenty? You don't mean that?" It is his accent, I think, I must have misunderstood.

He writes me this figure down on a napkin, wet with the moisture from the bottom of a cocktail glass. It is twenty. "What do you do?"

"Computers. I program. Computers."

"But why so many jobs then?"

"I cannot get along." He shrugs, he makes a face. "The people I work with, they are incompetent, useless. Lazy bastards. I know how to do things. The know . . . nothing. It is impossible. I quit, I go somewhere else. But it is always the same story."

"It's their fault, never your own? That's what you're saying?"

He does not reply. He thinks it senseless to repeat what to him is patently obvious. "Lazy bastards," he repeats insistently after a long pause.

We stand, the two of us, overlooking our drinks with the contemplative air of philosophers who've temporarily suspended their dialogue. The silence is interminable. Georgio crimples his brow as if he is drawing on his memory. He is trying to remember something, an incident out of the past, an idea, an inspiration. His eyebrows suddenly arch, then settle back into place. The rigidity goes out of his face. He's got it now, he remembers.

He touches his fingers to my shoulder. He tilts his head closer to mine. He has a story to tell me from the looks of it, but he is careful that nobody overhears.

He begins: "Once I was seeing this lady. We had an affair, but it did not last long, not long at all. Then she wanted nothing to do with me. She did not return my telephone calls. I wrote her letters and she did not respond to them." He assumes an expression of anguished pride now; I must be made aware as to how painful this memory is to him. "One night I decide to go see her and convince her of my love. She was living then in an apartment on the tenth floor. I knew her building by heart, all the doors, all the stairways, no problem. I ring her bell but there is no answer. I see that her lights are out. But I do not go away. You know what I did?" He laughs and his laughter is pitched high, like a schoolboy's. "I go up to the roof. A simple matter. I come to the roof and from there I climb down into her window. So easy, so easy. The window is open. It was summer and I knew she kept the window open. I am not so dumb after all. You know what I do?"

I tell him that I have no idea. He is exultant, gulps his drink down, and resumes: "I take off all of my clothes, yes, all of them, and I get into her bed. How well I know this bed! Then I stretch out and wait for her to return. Some hours go by and then I see it is nearly dawn. But she comes back and with her is a man. A big man, broad shoulders. She turns on the lights and gives a look at me. And you know, she screams. She is so angry. 'What are you doing here?' she asks me. 'What are you doing here? How did you get in here? Get out of here!' I tell her the truth. I say through the window, that's how I get in. She turns to her boyfriend, she says, 'What are you going to do about him? What are you going to do about him?'

"But he does not know what to do. He says this is her problem, he is not going to get involved. So he sits down on a chair in the corner. She is more angry with him than with me, you know? She fumes and frets, then she comes to me and she gets on the bed and tries to get me to leave. I am stronger than she is. I am laughing. This is too much for her. She pulls, she pushes, she does everything. I am not budging. It is too much. She is laughing too. She doesn't want to laugh, she just can't help herself. And all the time there is her boyfriend, he is still sitting over in the corner, watching everything. But doing nothing. Finally he just gets up and goes out without saying a thing. She is too busy laughing to notice." Georgio scrutinizes me, his eyes glistening. "You know what happens? You can guess now?"

"I can guess," I say, but that is all.

Georgio continues to chuckle to himself. I feel compelled to intrude on his happy memory. "Where is she now, this girl?"

He opens his hands to the stale air. "Gone, gone. Now it is terrible. No women. Impossible to climb into bedrooms from rooftops. Too many muggers, too many murderers, too many rapists. Not enough lovers. Before, it is so simple, so easy. I go up to a woman on a street and no trouble. Now you talk to them, they won't listen. Too suspicious. The murderers, the muggers, the rapists . . ." His voice trails off.

He seems about to leave. He stoops to retrieve his briefcase. Though he only carries a magazine or two in this briefcase, it is important somehow for him to be seen with it; maybe it gives him the sense that he is a man of some significance. In his pathetic way he must reassure me: "I am not gay, you know. I just wished to talk."

Georgio is unrelenting. He finds me in my dreams as he does in my waking state. I am convinced for a time that I must be exuding a strange odor that only Georgio is capable of picking up on, and consequently I spend hours in the shower. It does no good, of course. He still finds me. I may be in the middle of a park or standing in line outside a movie theater. Perhaps I am in a tavern where I have never been before or else surrounded by tourists on a ferry. It does not seem to matter to him. He is like one of those faithful dogs you read about, the ones who having been abandoned in New York somehow make their way unerringly to their old masters in California. How do they know? How do birds know when to migrate, which direction to pursue? They know, they know, that's all.

Eventually I grow so resentful of Georgio's recurrences that I begin—foolishly perhaps—to blame him for my troubles. As summer comes to its midpoint, I find that I am without a job. For nearly a year I had been a copywriter for a trade magazine. But now due to various personality differences I'd been fired, with only an afternoon to clear my desk. I did not like my job, there was no future in it; still I am oddly bitter to lose it in this manner. As it is summer, most of my friends are away, lolling about vacation resorts. I imagine that their lives are untroubled and radiant, full of new liaisons, daiquiris, sailboats, and water skiing. I am alone, standing in unemployment lines, wandering on dazed afternoons through the city where sidewalks buckle and asphalt cracks.

Wrong: I am not alone, I have Georgio.

Perhaps I am exaggerating. Because the fact is I do have a friend, a woman named Toni, who I know from work. Unfortunately, the position she occupies in my life is that of a companion, nothing more. Her love, she says, is far away, and yet she persists in remaining faithful to him. She expects to go to him one day soon. I lie and tell her that I too have a love of my own who is far away. She never realizes that the distance I am referring to is not one measured in miles. Thus we deceitfully console one another.

Toni is attractive, I suppose, though somewhat on the plump side. Still her legs taper well and grow easily tan with all those long weekend afternoons spent sunbathing on her roof. It was possible to learn the story of her life in one sitting: there was, for instance, an abortion two years back, a few erratic and unsuccessful affairs; her present man was someone with three children and an unloved wife, all of whom live in a remote part of Scandinavia; there were certain eccentricities about her parents, too, which are not necessary to go into here. In other words, Toni's story is nothing extraordinary, nothing that couldn't be duplicated by a woman in similar circumstances down the block or maybe in the next apartment.

Toni knows all there is to know of Georgio long before meeting him. And because we spend so much time together it is inevitable that she will meet him. And so she does, the encounter finally occurring in the murky atmosphere of a downtown pub paneled in wood that looks more expensive than it probably is. Unwittingly, Toni selects a stool at the bar located next to the one Georgio has taken.

It is the same now. Perhaps it is worse. His eyes gleam, bright with the lusty memory of rooftops and bedrooms. He motions to me, his manner is secretive as always. He whispers into my ears. Toni has only to take one look at him before turning away in disgust; without any introduction, she realizes who he is. And already she doesn't care for him. There is no likelihood she will listen in on what he has to say; she doesn't want to hear.

"I know a place," he begins. "I will give you an address."

"What's at this address?"

His voice retreats another octave. I can barely comprehend him. "A woman."

"A whore you mean?'"

"A whore, yes. I will give you the address. I know her very well. We have a . . . special relationship."

Georgio is sincere, naive, and devious all at the same time. When I inform him that his proposition does not interest me, he expresses his puzzlement. "It is a *special* relationship," he insists, but to no avail.

He decides on a different tack. He will ignore me and concentrate on Toni. "What are you doing tomorrow evening?" he asks, his fingers poised in the air above her shoulder.

Annoyed, she replies, "I'm busy, I've got plans."

"Saturday night? What about next Saturday night?"

He is absolutely undeterred by my presence. It is an amazing performance.

"No, not then. I'm all booked up. Whichever day you name, I'm booked up."

He shrugs, a monumental shrug, but still he remains impervious. In a few moments he has come up with another approach. "Do you like gold, by the way?"

"No, no, I don't like gold. Silver, but not gold."

"Because I have some gold. Very cheap. Gold earrings, gold bracelets. Fifteen dollars the earrings. I have a friend. I can get them for you. Cheap, no? Fifteen dollars."

"I told you I don't like gold. I don't want any gold."

He falls silent. Is it possible that we have gotten through to him? Already he registers dismay, hurt; he must be thinking that I, his friend, have humiliated him. This he cannot understand. "I am bored," he suddenly announces. "There is nothing for me here. I am going home."

We say good-bye, a perfunctory farewell, and he, still looking very unhappy, is last seen as a blur of a black coat slipping out through the door with a big red Exit sign overhead.

Georgio is not gone. He remains in our dominions, but this time he has evidently transferred his allegiance—if that is what it is—to Toni. Within the week she will hear a voice, hoarse and unidentifiable, call to her from a doorway. She turns to see him popping up, a comic figure, with wild eyes and pouting lips. He must remind her as to who he is, what he is about. "I am Georgio. We met before. In the bar. I have been having dreams about you and your friend every night since I saw you."

Frightened, but more surprised than frightened, Toni backs away, flees down the street, listening for the sound of pursuing footsteps. There are none. Georgio does not follow, does not need to follow; he knows where she will next be.

In another part of the city he will again corner her. There is nothing overtly threatening about him. He stands there like a hapless bum, a slob in a worn trenchcoat, frazzled at the edges. His hands are in his pockets, his head is hung almost as if in apology for what he is obliged to say. "My name is Georgio," he ritualistically proclaims, "My name is Georgio. Do you remember me? We met in a bar two weeks ago. I have dreams about you every night since I saw you. I have dreams about you and your friend . . . I think you are wonderful together. I wish to be a slave to you and your friend."

Toni retreats from him, warily, one foot, then the other. "You're everywhere," she says, and he smiles with this acknowledgment of his ubiquity. It is not rape, it is not mutilation or even murder which scares her now, no, it is his mere touch which she dreads so very much.

He refuses to obey her when she orders him to leave, and yet he approaches no further. He stands where he is, the source of some disagreeable kitchen odor. He scrutinizes her carefully, methodically, as she flushes, then pales, as she becomes damp with perspiration, as her hands tremble against her will.

Soon Toni blames Georgio just as I had previously. Her father falls ill and her sister requires an abortion, her mother is suddenly distant with her over the phone, and her friends at work won't confide in her any longer, it is all Georgio's fault. Her job may even be in jeopardy, she says, and again it is Georgio's doing. "I know I can't prove it but you know it's true."

"I agree with you. I feel the same way," I answer.

Toni swears she will murder Georgio, but instead she procures a canister of Mace, which she takes with her wherever she goes. "Just let him come near me, just let him raise a finger . . ."

Whatever method of communication Georgio relies upon, whatever psychic transmittal service it is, he soon knows enough to keep his distance. He will never come close enough for her to wield her spray of irritant gas. Rather he will yell to her from across the street or appear on a fire escape over her head and well out of range. Before she can bring herself to respond he has already disappeared, vanishing among the pollutants of our city.

As her troubles grow worse, Toni begins to drink more. At times I think she is drinking to forget Georgio. On other occasions I know this is not true, I know that it is her distant love, the Scandinavian hero, who dominates her thoughts. We are spending still more time together. I accompany her from one bar to the next. She starts off her boozing in high enough spirits, she's giddy and talkative, but as the night wears on she inevitably becomes withdrawn, falling sullen and quietly enraged. She tries dancing but the room spins for her. She tries talking and touching hands and bodies to regain contact, but she cannot get anyone to respond as she would like them to. She is always astonished to find herself drunk.

I take her outside in hope of restoring her. The cold air, I think, should do it. It does not. She flops down as soon as I loosen my hold on her and winds up sitting in a ridiculous posture on the curbstone. I hoist her back up and hail an oncoming cab.

"You'll stay with me?" she pleads, almost tearful. "You'll stay with me, won't you? I am going to be sick, I just know it. I need to have somebody stay with me." She may be drunk, but her words are not slurred, she is careful to pronounce each one distinctly so that there should be no misunderstanding.

"I'll stay," I assure her.

By the time we reach her apartment building some twenty minutes later, she says she feels better. And it's true she doesn't look quite as pale. "You don't have to hold onto me. I can walk by myself." She walks fast, stamps her feet with impatience when the elevator is delayed. "God, I've got to pee," she cries out, loud enough so that the doorman can hear her. She may think that the demands of her bladder are sufficiently powerful to bring the elevator down to earth.

When we stand by her door I am the one who has to work the key into the lock. She is unable to cope. Scarcely have I gotten the door open than she has scurried off to the bathroom, slamming the door behind her. Relief.

I notice that the apartment is completely dark. Odd. Generally she is sure to leave at least one light burning when she goes out at night. Now I know something is not right. Someone else is with us in the apartment. He lies in the bed, covered only by a single pink silk sheet.

Toni emerges from the bathroom and sees him for the first time. She is too aghast to utter a sound. Her mouth gapes open. When she is at last capable of speech she shrieks out, "Well, for God's sakes, do something!" She cannot manage to stand any longer and collapses in a chair. She sighs painfully.

I go over to him, not knowing what I am about to do. Certainly I must do something, take some action.

"You came from the roof," I say in a very conversational manner. "You got in through the window." Actually I don't know, but I think this the most likely possibility. He smiles indifferently but says nothing.

"You've got to get out of the bed," I say calmly. I find the prospect of persuading him, of coaxing him out of Toni's linen, a weirdly fascinating one. I hold up his discarded trousers, his undershorts full of holes. He does not react.

He says not a word, he enjoys our dilemma too much to want to speak. I reach down, grab him by his wrists, but his skin is unexpectedly smooth, oiled in sweat, and my hold falters. For all my exertions I can make no headway, he simply will not be budged. I pull, I twist, I lift one hand away, ready to hit him squarely in the solar plexus, but at the last moment he turns and deflects my attack. When I try again to hit him I find that he has seized hold of me. We are stalemated. No matter which way we move in an attempt to attain a superior position, neither of us can hope to win.

It is only now that I turn around to see how Toni is doing. But she is not there. She might have gone for help. Maybe she just couldn't stand the sight of us.

"If it's her you want she's not here, can't you see?"

But Georgio greets this news impassively. It may be that he has only used her to get to me, that I am the one he really wants. But what can I do? I am immobilized, pinned in his hold. How was I to know that Georgio was so powerful, so incredibly strong? The diminutiveness and thinness of his body were a deception.

There is no escaping him now.

As if he is capable of deciphering my thoughts he laughs, and in order that I will know for the next time, he says, "That's how it is. I get nothing . . . so you get nothing too."

People are terrible weapons. Their less than honorable character-
istics (what English teachers call "tragic flaws") are more often
than not kept under control, consciously or not. But there are
times when control is lost, and words more than deeds cause
irreparable harm to seemingly innocent bystanders. Bleeding
externally is not nearly so lethal as bleeding from the soul.

Wayne Wightman's stories are just now beginning to appear in
the major sf and fantasy magazines, and his notion of what a
shadow is, is perhaps more deadly than others.

THE TOUCH

by Wayne Wightman

She wondered if Chas would die if she went out to dinner with
him. This is what she thought as she drew a careful brown line
above the darkened eyelashes of her left eye. Her eyes were the
eyes of a forty-year-old, although Arlene Brown was only twenty-
nine. Bad genes, she supposed.

She supposed it would probably be safe to let Chas take her to
dinner. Maybe she could let him kiss her good-night. She leaned
back from the mirror and checked her work. That's the best
Arlene Brown can look, she thought. She had the most common
straight brown hair. It had to be tortured to hold the vaguest
wave. Her thin lips rarely expressed anything but tenseness, and
her nose was thickish and freckled. Yet men wanted her. Always.
Always men wanted her. Chas wanted her.

She did not want men much. Not much. Just sometimes, and
then quite a bit—in moderation. What she wanted was affection.
She liked to be hugged. She liked to have men like her. But a
terrible thing had happened three times now. During the last
two years, her last three boyfriends had died. One in a car wreck,
one got lost in the mountains in winter and wasn't found till
spring, and one had died of an exotic pneumonia while on a
business trip in the Philippines. So Arlene Brown packed all she
owned in three brown cartons and moved away. She moved to
Stockton, California, a place she had never heard of.

She worked in a department store. She sold men's clothes. That was where she met Chas. He had come in for a shirt and had left with five of them, a set of handkerchiefs, a vested suit, and underwear. And he left with a big smile. Arlene knew she would see him again.

That was when she began to worry. After Stephen had killed himself in his car and after Len had got lost in the mountains, Daniel had been there to comfort her. He hugged her. He liked her. He told her she was irrational in her guilt, that she could have had nothing to do with their deaths. Then Daniel died in Manila. They said he weighed only ninety-five pounds at the end, just what Arlene weighed. Not only was she plain, she was very thin. She felt tired all the time.

Arlene walked into her living room and sat in a soft blue chair. Rented chair. Rented furniture. Rented apartment. Back home, she was about to buy a house. But people seemed to look at her too much. Poor-poor-Arlene looks. And Len's and Daniel's parents always wanted her to come for dinner and talk about their sons. She did it for a while, but she couldn't do it anymore.

Her apartment was nice enough—for an apartment.

She looked up at the ceiling. Benny, who lived just above her, was pacing again. She did not care for Benny. Benny worked at a stereo store. Two or three times a week he would call her or knock at her door or meet her on the stairs or talk to her at the supermarket. He would nervously bite at his lips and ask her things about men's clothing—what was a chambray shirt, or what was the difference between a twill and a tweed? Sometimes he tried to give her records. Although he would never look her in the eyes, Arlene knew what he was looking for. She tried to be kind in refusing his gifts and in answering his questions.

Arlene looked at her wristwatch. Chas could arrive any time. She hoped her mascara would not make her eyes red. She hoped she would not get sleepy during dinner either. She had been getting more and more tired lately, without any good reason for it. Hugging would help. That would help a lot. If Chas would hug her, she would feel a lot better.

There was a light tap at her door.

Arlene took a deep breath and stood up and brushed the wrinkles out of the lap of her pants. Now she was going to start feeling better, she told herself. She and Chas would have a nice dinner with a nice wine and he might hold her hand, and later he would hug her, and she would go to bed, alone, feeling much better.

She opened the door. It was Benny. He wore a white shirt, tie, and slacks, but his clothes looked heavy with oil. He bit into the back of his lower lip and stared nervously down the hall; he never looked at her. "You shouldn't go out with that guy," Benny said. He put his hands in his pockets.

"What?" Arlene said.

"You shouldn't go out with that guy," Benny said again. "Just take my word for it."

Arlene looked at Benny. She didn't know what to think, but she was starting to feel angry. "How do you know I'm going out with *any*one?"

Benny rocked side to side on his feet. He seemed to be looking at the ceiling some distance down the hall. "I know you're going out with Chas tonight, all right? I'm just trying to save you some difficulty, you know, that could result from you going out with that guy. No big deal or anything, you know. Just trying to do you a favor." He rocked back and forth on his feet.

Arlene cleared her throat. "I appreciate your concern for my welfare," she said, trying to smile politely, "but I don't appreciate your expression of it."

"Listen, I know you think I'm a creep. I'm a nervous guy, I apologize. What else can I say? Trying to do you a favor. This Chas guy, he's married. I thought you should know."

"He's separated."

"Oh."

"Don't check on him anymore, Benny. And if you've been listening at my door, stop it. I really don't like it. That isn't one of the ways a person gets to be my friend."

Benny was nodding in an exaggerated motion. Then he looked at the floor near his feet. "I knew you'd take it this way. I just knew the hell out of it. Well." He looked up at the ceiling and took his hands out of his pockets. "Just thought I'd try to help. You just remember, though, if anything happens to old Chas, you know, if he was to get in a car wreck or freeze to death in some parking lot or catch some weird disease, you just remember old Benny-the-Creep lives just up the stairs and you can always get some understanding and some good herb tea from old Benny-the-Creep. Can you remember that?"

"You've been spying on me," Arlene said slowly. "Why are you doing this to me?"

"Look, I'm not trying to make your life miserable or anything. I'm not *that* kind of jerk."

Arlene felt tears coming into her eyes. "But you *are* making my life miserable!" Her lips got very tense and hardly moved when she talked. "Please leave me alone. *Please* don't spy on me."

He turned away from her a little more. He stared unmoving at his feet. "It's just a superstition you got, that's all," he mumbled. "It's just bad luck about what happened." He glanced at her and then turned away again. She could barely hear him. "You could like me. I'd like it if you liked me. Instead of Chas."

"Please don't talk to me again," Arlene said. "I appreciate your concern, but I would prefer it if you stopped thinking about me. Good-bye."

"Right," Benny said. He began walking away, toward the stairs. "Right. Got the message loud and clear on all wavelengths." He was still talking when Arlene closed the door.

Even here, she thought, strangers remind me of it.

In the space of a minute her aura of privacy had been penetrated by a stranger who happened to live near her. If things had gone well, she might have told Chas some of the secret things about herself—it was to Chas she wanted to reveal herself, not to a stranger, not to Benny-the-Creep.

Arlene went into the bathroom and washed her hands. She was drying them when the doorbell rang. She stuffed the towel into the rack, went to the door, and pressed the buzzer to let him in the downstairs entryhall. While she waited for him to come up, she went back to the bathroom and straightened the hand towel. A quick glance in the mirror told her that all her making up was for nothing; her lips were tight, her eyes red, and her mascara had smeared onto one eyelid. It made her want to cry.

Chas knocked and she opened the door. She stood back and tried to smile, but that made it worse. Her eyes burned. She didn't see him reach toward her; she only felt his arms wrapping around her and his big hands seeming to cover half her back as he held her close against him. His suit smelled of cloth and cologne. She cried for a minute, and then she managed to stop.

Chas turned his head down so that his lips were close to her ear. "At least," he said, "I know you're not crying because of something I said."

She tried to shake her head. "No," she said wetly.

He kissed her on her cheek, through a spread of her hair. "Is this your way of saying you'd rather not go out to dinner?"

"No, it isn't that. It isn't anything you did." She pulled back and looked up at him. He had dark hair and fine strong bones in his face; she couldn't imagine why a man so good looking would choose to go out with her. "You shouldn't kiss me," Arlene said. She put her cheek against his chest again because she didn't want to look at him or to explain.

"I'd like to know what's happened," Chas said, "but you don't have to tell me anything if you don't want to."

"Just hug me real tight."

His hands seemed to spread wider across her back. She could feel the tension in her stomach and face begin to ease. She was glad he was here. "I've cried on your suit," she said.

"Doesn't matter." With one hand he touched her hair and then pressed her face against him.

"I'm all right now." She took a deep breath. "I'm almost all right now. We can go sit down if you want." When she looked up at him, he was smiling a little.

He took her face in his hands and kissed her lips. She saw what he was going to do and she wanted to draw away, but she didn't . . . she didn't and she liked it.

"I'd like to sit down," Chas said. He let her go and turned and picked up a large paper bag from the floor. From it he first took a foil-topped bottle. "I'd like to sit down with you and two glasses."

Arlene realized she was gripping her hands together in front of her; she let them fall to her sides. "I'm sorry," she said, "I didn't see you bring that in." For some reason she felt like she might cry again.

He must have noticed because he put one arm around her. Offering her the bottle, he said, "I got this for us because I wanted you to like me the minute I walked in the door."

She took it in her hands. "I did like you the minute you walked in the door—even without this." His hand tightened on her shoulder a little.

Then he reached in the bag and brought out a bouquet of red carnations. "And I brought you these so you would remember me after I left."

The flowers were so red that they seemed to glow. She began to smile. "This is the first time anybody ever gave me flowers because they liked me. They're so red, and beautiful."

He turned her toward the kitchen. "Why did people give you flowers if they didn't like you?"

She looked at the label of the bottle as they walked. She wondered how one pronounced *Taittinger*. She wondered how she would answer his question and how much she would tell him.

"I got flowers at funerals."

He looked at her.

"Friends of mine have died. People gave me flowers for sympathy, I guess. Why don't you open this for us."

While Chas unclipped the wire and slowly turned the cork out, Arlene wrote him a note. It said,

> There is a man upstairs named Benny who knows that I'm going out with you tonight. I don't know how he found out. Maybe he is listening to us now.

Chas poured foaming white champagne into the two glasses. He handed her one and lightly touched the lips of the glasses together.

"Make a wish," he said softly.

"Do I have to say it out loud?"

"Never."

She thought about Benny and then smiled and nodded.

Chas was smiling and looking into her eyes as they drank. He saw the note, read it, and put it back on the counter. "Do you like this?" he asked about the champagne.

"Yes." She glanced at the note. "I'd probably enjoy it even more if I hadn't been . . . upset, just before you got here."

"Benny, you mean."

She stared at him.

"The man upstairs?"

"Yes," she said very softly.

"Did he come down here or phone you?"

"He came down. He'll hear you talking," she whispered.

"But it doesn't matter," Chas said. He leaned forward and kissed her lips lightly again. "If you don't mind, I'll check around and see what I can find, if anything." He grinned. "Just like in the movies." He put his glass down and went to the telephone and unscrewed the mouthpiece. "Maybe I can leave old Benny some kind of message. Ah, *just* like in the movies." He pointed into the receiver. Arlene moved toward him. "Message to Benny:" Chas said into the telephone. "I am a friend of Arlene's, and when I arrived this evening she was very upset as a result of your visit and your eavesdropping. You've interfered in my personal life, Benny. You may have ruined what I had expected to be a wonderful evening. Don't interfere in my life, Ben. It makes me hostile. It makes me want to kick your nuts up around your neck. You get my general drift, Benny? Take a hint."

Arlene felt herself stiffen at what Chas said—but he was doing it to protect her, almost like he was giving her a different kind of hug. Chas had removed the round object from the receiver and was screwing the cover back on when Arlene put her arms around him again.

"Chas," she said, smelling the cloth and cologne, "let's stay here this evening. I don't think I could eat or be very comfortable out in public after all this. We have the flowers and champagne." She looked up at him. "And I need to talk to someone."

He put his hands around her face. They were warm and dry, and his hands like that made her feel helpless and held and protected. Then he kissed her.

Chas sat in the corner of the sofa and Arlene lay with her cheek on his chest. One of his arms ran the length of her torso and his hand rested on the swell of her hips. Sometimes when he talked he moved his hand, and fingers would brush against the inside of her leg. She told him how she had learned from her lawyer father to put work before pleasure and how she had done it and was still a virgin. She told him about Stephen and Len and Daniel and why she had moved to Stockton. "That's why I didn't want you to kiss me," she said. "I don't want anything to happen to you."

Chas reached to a small table and emptied the champagne into their glasses. "Well." He kissed the top of her head. "I've already told you how dangerous you seem to me."

"Something else that worries me . . . is that I can't seem to like a man for very long until it all gets . . . *normal* again. Flat-feeling. It was only with Stephen, Len, and Daniel . . ."

"You can tell me. I'm not going to be hurt."

"I really thought I was in love with them," she said. "I guess I *was* in love with them. They're the only ones I ever thought that about. But toward the end, I felt myself drifting away from them. I didn't need to see them very much to be satisfied—there were other things I wanted to spend time on. It happened so gradually that I hardly noticed when I started easing them out of my life." She lifted her head and sipped the champagne. "I could get used to this," she said as she swallowed. "It was very expensive, wasn't it?"

Chas smiled.

She put her glass down and lay against him and hugged him. She liked very much his smell and the solidness of his chest. "Do you think there might be something wrong with me? That I can't like anyone for very long before it goes all flat-feeling?"

"That happens to everyone. You haven't met the right person."

"I'm afraid that if I did meet the right person, he'd die." Her hands tightened on him. She wanted to be hugged. She wanted that badly. "It makes me awfully afraid," she said. "I try to be light about it, and I make myself scared."

He held her with both arms. She felt like a child in its father's protection. "Listen to me now," he said softly. His voice was deep and rumbly in his chest. "Listen—anyone who had gone through what you've gone through would think there was some kind of cause and effect operating there. But there couldn't have been. Regardless of how it appears, the rational parts of us know that those men didn't die because you loved them. Or because they loved you. That just doesn't happen."

"But maybe it did."

"If it *did* happen, then you know how to make Benny stop bothering you—you have a secret weapon. If it didn't happen, if there was no cause and effect, then you can have me for as long as we want." He kissed the top of her head.

She closed her eyes and breathed in his smell and his solidness and the ease of his thinking.

"The day I met you," he said, "I started thinking about you. At first it seemed odd that I couldn't get you out of my mind. When I thought of you, I thought of your eyes. I love your eyes."

"They're old-looking and small."

"I love your eyes. The second time I saw you, I didn't go away just thinking about you—I went away wanting you."

With her cheek still on his chest, she reached up and touched his lips with her fingers. "Maybe you shouldn't say any more." She breathed him in. She wanted him to hold her a long time.

"I want you, and I want to need you."

She drew herself up so she could look into his face. "You make it seem so easy. You make it seem like I should love you."

He kissed her and she lay against him with his arms around her, and sometimes they talked. Sometimes he kissed her, and whenever he did, she felt like he was draining away her loneliness and replacing it with bits and pieces of himself. She became warm and sleepy.

He kissed her good-night and left with the promise of calling her in the afternoon.

Arlene Brown turned on her electric blanket and pulled the covers up to her chin. She felt better than she had in months. Someone had entered her life again, someone who would do things for her, who would make some of the small decisions about how she should spend her time and how she should do things, and he was someone she could do things for, also. He filled her thoughts.

When she slept, she dreamed of Benny. She dreamed she was driving a mountain road, and Benny, in another car, was trying to edge her off into the canyon and into the river at the bottom, far below. There was a crash, like the sides of two cars slamming together, and Arlene bolted upright in bed—but the dream went on another one or two seconds, and she had the feeling that one of the cars went off the cliff. She sat there blinking her eyes, the blankets gathered around her waist, wondering if Benny's car had flown off the cliff into the river, or if it had been hers. Sweat broke out across her hairline.

She lay awake, staring at the ceiling. She wanted to think of Chas, but she could only think of Benny.

Arlene looked at her eyes in the mirror. If I could just get some sleep, she thought, I'd look a lot better. There was a tapping at her door. She hurried to answer it, thinking Chas could have decided to come by without calling. But as she put her hand on the latch, she realized that Chas would not do that—and as she pulled the door open, she was resigning herself to face the person she knew it had to be.

"Good morning, Arlene."

"Good morning, Benny." She felt the old tiredness coming back in waves. "What do you want?"

"I just wanted to see that you're all right."

She stared at him a moment before answering. His hair was not carefully combed this morning. He rocked back and forth a little on his feet. "I'm fine," she said. "We found the thing you put in the telephone. Do you also listen to what goes on in my living room?"

"I'm just trying to watch out for you," he said, looking up at the hall ceiling. "You trust people too much. I don't want anything happening to you. It's not a safe neighborhood."

Arlene stared at him. The corner of his mouth twitched. He looked at the floor and stuffed his hands into his jacket pockets. He sniffed.

She stared at him, and he started to say something else, but he looked at her instead. He looked away quickly, and then looked back. It seemed to Arlene that he had soft eyes, almost as though they were lacking pressure and could be very easily hurt.

"Why don't you come in for a few minutes," she said. "Come in and I'll fix you some tea." She closed the door behind him.

Benny was shy at first, but then he began to talk. He told her, again, that he was only concerned for her welfare. Arlene said she understood. He told her of his scattered family and how, of all his siblings, only he was not a professional. He wept a little, and she was sympathetic. A family, he said, was something he had begun to miss, and he imagined that Arlene could provide him with a closeness he said he had never had. He wept again, was embarrassed, and Arlene went over to his chair and knelt beside it. She put her hand over his.

"You make it seem so easy," she said. "You make it seem like I *should* love you."

She heard him catch his breath. His eyes looked as delicate as snowflakes.

"But I have to go now," she said gently. "I'm supposed to meet a girlfriend for lunch." She watched him for any reaction—there was none; perhaps he only listened to her phone conversations.

Benny got to his feet. His clothes were wrinkled from sitting. "Can I call you later today?" he asked timidly.

"I may be out late," she said, smiling, "but do call, yes." She touched his chest with one finger as he walked out the door. She felt creepy with disgust.

She phoned Chas from a booth and arranged to meet him for a late breakfast. Over crepes and sour cream and strawberries, they talked about places they liked to go for vacations. Arlene did not mention Benny once. At the first sight of Chas, all unpleasant thoughts vanished. He was what she needed, what she wanted, what made her feel good again about being Arlene Brown. They talked about Yosemite and Santa Cruz and Mount Shasta and Tahoe. They talked about going away together.

Through the sliding glass doors at the foot of the bed, they watched the rain. The narrow balcony of weathered redwood glistened. Beyond the balcony, the rain fell on the salt marsh where seabirds rose and spiraled erratically. Hidden in the gray air, the ocean, just beyond the marsh, frothed at the sand.

"This wasn't what I was thinking of when we planned this," Chas said.

She knew he was not talking about the weather. "It's all right," she said. "Just rest. If you don't feel well, we shouldn't try to go anywhere today." Chas was under the blankets; Arlene lay on top of the bedcovers. She wore tweed pants and a cable-knit sweater. She tucked the blankets close to his shoulders and neck. "I like being with you, whatever the situation."

"We'll go out for dinner," Chas said. He shook his head. "This is typical of my luck," he said. "The best thing that's happened to

me in years . . . planned for three months . . . and then . . ."
He shrugged his shoulders under the blankets.

Arlene tucked them back in and touched him on the cheek and
said, "It isn't your fault." She went to the mirror over the dressing table and looked at her eyes. They looked better. She was
sleeping better these days.

Behind her, Chas said, "I haven't heard you mention your
neighbor in quite a while. Benny his name? Does he still call you
or meet you in the hallway?"

"Oh no. He called for a while, but I always managed to be
busy." She ran a finger under her left eye. The skin was smooth
and firm. "Using all my feminine charm, I asked him to take his
listening devices out of his floor, and he did."

"The power of beauty," Chas murmured.

"Oh yes," she said grinning. "Arlene Brown, the unendurable
beauty."

"You're more beautiful than I can say," Chas said softly.

Arlene ran her finger under her right eye. There wasn't a trace
of darkness there. "I told Benny that he and I had no future." She
stood up and crossed to the sliding glass doors. Out in the drizzle,
white birds rose from the marsh in parabolas and then dived back
into the wet gray foliage. "I told him that regardless of my personal feelings for him, my work and my family took up all my
time and emotional energy." Her breath fogged up an oval spot
on the glass.

"I've never known anyone like you before," Chas whispered
from the bed. "I didn't know I could be so much in love with
someone . . . that being away from you for just a day could . . .
be so painful."

She lay again on the bed beside him. "I never want to hurt
you," she said. "You've been so good to me. You've given me so
much." She kissed his forehead. She held him.

"I was hoping we could make love on this trip," he said. "I
hoped this would be the time."

She kissed his forehead.

"Do you still love me?" he asked.

"I'll always love you," she said. She wanted to wash her hands.

They watched the drizzle. Past the glistening balcony a hundred birds rose in unison out of the marsh and vanished in the

misty air. It rained until dark. When it became light, even the marsh was hidden in fog.

The walls and bed were white. The roses she had brought and placed on the bedside table looked too red. They looked bright.

"We've always told each other the truth," he said. "We've always believed what the other said."

Arlene nodded. She knew he was going to ask her, and she knew she would tell him. She always told him the truth, as she had told Stephen, Len, and Daniel the truth.

"There isn't much room in your life for me, is there?" he asked.

She looked down. "I enjoy my work. I could be promoted if I do well." She looked up at him. "You know that's important to me."

"Do you think—" He started coughing. Arlene was reaching for the button to signal the nurse when he stopped. "Do you think, when I get out of here, we could see each other a little more than we have been?"

She looked at her hands. "Why don't we—"

"I understand." Only his lips moved. "You don't have to explain, really. You don't have to. It isn't my business now."

"I'll always love you," she said.

A siren passed in the street below. When it was quiet again, Chas said, "I had hoped we could see summer together."

She kissed his forehead. It was cold and moist.

There was a light tapping at her door. She had been cleaning her apartment. She wore Levi's, an old plaid shirt of her father's with the sleeves rolled up, and a bandana around her hair. She wasn't sure she wanted to be seen by anyone. She opened the peephole.

The man was familiar in some way, but she was sure she had never seen him before.

"I'm the brother of Benny Pedrakis, your neighbor upstairs. He mentioned you and I just wanted to ask you a couple of things about him."

She opened the door. The man was shorter than Benny and his eyes were very hard. His suit was richly textured and expensive-looking.

"I'm going to sit down," he said, heading for the armchair.

"Please do," Arlene said. "Exactly what is it you want to know?"

The man sat down and put his arms on the arms of the chair and curled his fingers down over the front edge. "Exactly what I want to know," he said, staring at her, "is just what the fuck *are* you?"

Arlene felt herself tensing up. Her mouth became very tight.

"My brother, Benny, he's gone, you know? *Gone.* Three weeks ago he called his mother. All she can tell me is that he was real depressed over some woman. His angel, he called her. So I go to his apartment, and I find all these tapes and logbooks stacked up to the ceiling." The man's eyes opened wider and he shook his head in a little quivering motion. "You know what they were all about? About you, young woman, and about the other men who died because of you."

Arlene thought she was going to cry. "I don't know anything about Benny. I haven't seen him in over a month. I never had anything to do with him."

"Hah," the man said, slapping one hand on the chair arm. "Bullshit. I heard that conversation. He had himself wired every time he talked to you. You led him on. *You led him on,* and now, where is he? Huh?"

She held her cheeks with her hands; they were hot. Tears ran between her fingers. "I don't know where he is. I don't know what happened to him. I don't know anything about him."

"What about your friend Chas?" the man said with an unpleasant smile. "Do you know where Chas is? Tell me where your friend Chas is?"

She couldn't speak. The knot in her throat was suffocatingly huge. She shook her head. "Please. . . . I don't know why these things happen to me." Her voice was so small she wasn't sure he heard her.

"Your friend Chas is out making wormfood, isn't he. Benny had the clippings for all of your dead friends. How much did your friend Chas leave you? Hm? This looks like new furniture."

Arlene hid her face in her hands. "I can't talk—" She went behind the kitchen counter and took a towel off a rack and pressed it to her face.

The man walked over to the counter and leaned his stomach

against it. "You see," he said, "I know you killed my brother. I know you did that. I think you probably snuffed the other four too, but I don't care about them. What I care about is Benny. Where'd you dump him, huh? Aside from seeing to it that you get put away, we'd like to have Benny buried with the rest of his family."

Arlene's eyes burned. She wiped her eyes and nose on the towel.

"Mr. Pedrakis, I'll tell you everything I know. I don't understand why these things happen to me." She took the towel with her and sat in the corner of the sofa. She told him the truth.

After a while, she said, "Would you like me to make some tea or coffee?"

He wanted coffee, black.

When she handed him the filled cup, he said, "You have lovely hands."

The compliment embarrassed her. She thanked him. Later, she poured him a second cup.

Arlene Brown leaned her elbows on the windowsill and breathed in the summer-evening air. Below, on the sidewalks, people out for walks wore shorts and short-sleeved shirts. There were few cars. The evening was quiet.

Sometimes Arlene Brown hated herself. Other times she felt strong enough to live her life alone, without intimacy. Sometimes creeping loneliness hung around her like gauze.

She let her eyes travel far up the sidewalk and back down to the opposite end. Fifty or more people casually strolled along the street and looked in store windows.

Sometimes she felt a nervous mixture of self-loathing and excitement when she thought of herself in the embrace of a man who loved her. Sometimes she went to sleep thinking of a man, thinking of men. Of the fifty people on the sidewalk, more than half were men.

Sometimes she hated herself for what happened, but now, as she looked down at the street, she thought of men . . . all the men. She had been so tired lately, and there were so many men.

On the journey from childhood to adolescence to maturity, one's Critters have too often turned out to be fanciful shadows with no substance at all. But on that same journey, it's occasionally the case that a critter really is a Critter after all.

Marc Laidlaw is a West Coast writer, young enough to have more years ahead of him than those of us who started late, and an increasingly deft touch with the razor's edge.

SNEAKERS

by Marc Laidlaw

What are you dreaming, kid?

Oh, don't squeeze your eyes, you can't shut me out. Rolling over won't help—not that blanket either. It might protect you from monsters but not from me.

Let me show you something. Got it right here. . . .

Well look at that. Is it your mom? Can't you see her plain as day? Yeah, well try moonlight. Cold and white, not like the sun, all washed out; a five-hundred-thousandth of daylight. It can't protect you.

She doesn't look healthy, kid. Her eyes are yellow, soft as cobwebs—touch them and they'll tear. Her skin is like that too, isn't it? No, Mom's not doing so good. Hair all falling out. Her teeth are swollen, black, and charred.

Yeah, something's wrong.

You don't look so good yourself, kiddo—

"Mom . . . ?"

What if she doesn't answer?

Louder this time: "Mom!"

Brent sat up, wide-awake now, sensing the shadows on the walls taking off like owls in flight. And that voice. He could still hear it. Were those rubber footsteps running away down the alley, a nightmare in tennis shoes taking off before it was caught? He could still see his mother's face, peeling, rotten, dead.

Why wouldn't she answer?

He knew it was only a dream, she just hadn't heard him calling, tied up in her own dreams. A dream like any other. Like last night, when he had seen his father burning up in an auto wreck, broken bones coming through the ends of his chopped-off arms; and the night before that, an old memory of torturing a puppy, leaving it in the street where it got hit and squashed and spilled. And the night before? Something bad, he knew, though he couldn't quite capture it.

Every night he had come awake at the worst moments. Alone, frightened of the dream's reality, of the hold it had on the dark corners of his waking world. If that voice had whispered when he was awake, he knew the walls might melt and bulge, breathing, as the blankets crawled up his face and snaked down his throat, suffocating him. That voice knew all his secrets, it whispered from a mouth filled with maggots, fanged with steel pins, a slashed and twisting tongue.

How did it know him?

Brent lay back and watched the dark ceiling until it began to spin, and he felt himself drifting back to sleep. Everything would be safe now, the voice had run away, he would have okay dreams. At least until tomorrow night.

It was not fear, the next night, that kept him from sleeping. Curiosity. He stuffed pillows beneath his covers to create an elongated shape, then he sat on the floor inside his closet with a flashlight. He had drunk a cup of instant coffee after dinner, to help him stay awake.

He heard the clock downstairs chiming eleven; sometime later the television went off and the shower splashed briefly in his parents' bathroom. Midnight passed. A car went through the alley, though its headlights could not reach him in the closet.

At one o'clock, a cat's meow.

The sneakers came at two. Footsteps in the alley.

Brent nudged the door ajar and looked out at the pane of his window. He could see windows in the opposite house, a drooping net of telephone wires, the eye of a distant streetlight.

Footsteps coming closer. It could be just anyone. He thought he heard the squeak of rubber; it was such a real sound. This couldn't be the whisperer.

Then they stopped outside, just below his window. Not a sound did they make, for five minutes, ten, until he knew that he had fallen asleep and dreamed their approach, was dreaming even now, listening to his heart beating and a dog barking far away, and then the voice said, You're awake.

Brent pressed back into the closet, holding his flashlight as if it were a crucifix or a stake in a vampire movie. He didn't have a hammer, though.

Why don't you come out of there?

He shook his head, wishing that he were sound asleep now, where these whispers could only touch his dreams, could only make him see things. Not awake, like this, where if he took that talk too seriously, he knew the walls could melt.

I'm still here, kiddo. What did you wait up for?

Holding his flashlight clenched.

A walk, maybe?

He opened the closet door and crept out, first toward the bed, then toward the door of his room. Into the hall.

That's right.

Was he really doing this? No. It was a dream after all, because the hall was different, it wasn't the hall in his house: the paintings were of places that didn't exist, changing color, blobs of grey and blue shifting as if worms had been mashed on the canvases, were still alive. That wasn't his parents' door swinging wide, with something coming to look out. He mustn't look. There was a cage across the door so he was safe, but he mustn't look.

Downstairs, though, it was his living room. Dreams were like that. Completely real one minute, nonsense the next.

Like Alice in Wonderland. Like the Brothers Grimm or *Time Bandits.*

Who's real, kid? Not me. Not you. I promise.

Don't wake the White King.

Don't pinch yourself unless you want to know who's dreaming.

Don't open the back door and look into the alley, because here I am.

He turned on his flashlight.

Right behind you.

The black bag—if it was a bag—came down fast over Brent's eyes and whipped shut around his neck, smothering. He got lifted up and thrown across a bony shoulder. The sneakers started squeaking as he heard the alley gravel scatter.

Say bye-bye to Mommy and Daddy.

He was dreaming, this wasn't real.

There, that's what I meant, whispered the voice.

Depression, illness, any number or combination of things has let us imagine (for the sake of revenge or self-pity) that we were able to direct the circumstances of our own demise, or produce for private showing our own funerals. We get over it. Sometimes we even feel silly about having considered it in the first place. But we do it, because we also know it can't possibly happen.

Jack Dann lives in New York State and is both an award-nominated editor and writer; his work ably suggests that the ending of this story is not as gentle as it seems.

REUNION

by Jack Dann

It was a beautiful, blue Sunday morning, and Stephen Neshoma decided he would attend his own funeral.

He took a dip in his pool, which he did every morning, then showered, shaved, and dressed. He set the alarm system and stepped onto his circular driveway beside his two-year-old Lincoln Continental Town Car. He could see the bright surface segments of the intercoastal waterway between his neighbors' houses across the street, and he suddenly and sadly remembered his wife, Katharine, who had died a year after he left her. Stephen had no one to blame but himself.

His best friend, Leon, an orthopedic surgeon, had once referred to him as "the world's oldest adolescent"—Stephen was sixty-eight when he ran away to Florida with a young woman. In fact, he left Katharine just two days after his birthday. Now he had no wife . . . and his girlfriend had left him.

He got into the car and drove down Highway A-1A, past the pink steepled church, which most of his neighbors attended, past the thousand and one car dealerships, yacht outlets, shopping malls, restaurants, banks, and gas stations that gave character to the flatlands of Pompano and Ft. Lauderdale. He didn't drive to the funeral home, as viewing hours were over and he had requested a closed casket, anyway, but headed directly for the cemetery. Crowns Cemetery was very posh and well groomed and overlooked the beautiful Crowns Country Club, which was ultra-exclusive and had its own airfield where private Learjets sat like silver roaches.

At least I could afford to die properly, Stephen thought as he drove behind the funeral procession. A gray, dented Chevrolet was ahead of him, and it looked as if it was his cousin Myrna who was driving. So he got it right. This was the right procession and he was behind his favorite relative.

Everyone parked, and two attendants dressed in powder-blue tuxedos gently lifted Stephen's casket from a black Mercedes limousine. It was just a plain pine coffin, as he had requested.

Myrna got out of her car with her husband and three sons and they all, in turn, embraced Stephen's three surviving sisters: Cele, Kate, and Bess. Bess had just had another operation and wasn't feeling very well, although at seventy-eight, she could still get around. Bess and Kate and Cele lived together in an apartment in Brooklyn, and Bess and Kate fought all the time. Cele was a few years older than Stephen and still worked as a vice president of a burlap importing firm.

"Hello, Myrna," Cele said. She stood tall and stiff—she was certain that posture was important to long life—and proffered her cheek for a kiss. Her thin white hair was pulled back in a Gibson style and she wore a black crepe dress.

"Myrna should lose weight," Bess said to Kate in a whisper that could be heard by Myrna. Cele glowered at her sisters.

"I'm going to miss Stephen," Myrna said after she kissed Bess. Bess could stand to lose some weight herself.

"Yes, we'll all miss him," Cele said, as if filling in for Bess. "But it was his time and God took him. I only wish he hadn't made such a fool of himself with that *woman.*"

"He was afraid of getting old," Myrna said. Her husband, Don, who was tall and thin and fiftyish, nodded and said, "I'm afraid, too."

"But you wouldn't run away with a woman who's young enough to be your daughter," Cele said. "You wouldn't stop working and try to be a big shot."

"Who knows," Myrna said, giving Don a quick but nasty look. "He's not that old yet."

Bess started crying and Kate consoled her, but by then they

were all crying. Stephen, thinking that this was a good time to make himself known, walked over to them and asked how everyone was. He was wearing a classic cream suit, a brown striped tie, and white loafers. If he was going to be here, he thought, he might as well look natty.

As if on cue, Cele, Kate, and Bess stopped crying.

"So look who's decided to make an appearance," Kate said caustically. She wore a blue dress which complemented her dyed red hair. "We have to wait until you drop dead to see you. You couldn't have called, or taken a little time to see your sisters? They have planes between Florida and New York."

"You know how depressed I've been," Stephen said quietly. "It took me a long time to get over Susan. She hurt me very badly, she cut out my heart."

"Nonsense," Cele said. "She was a tramp, and you were a fool."

"You could have tried to understand. . . ."

"There was nothing to understand," Cele said. "And we were right, she left you high and dry, and instead of coming back to New York and spending your last years with us, you were too busy putting ads in the newspapers advertising for young girls. Do you think those young girls were interested in you because you're so handsome . . . ?"

"Well, he's always been a handsome man," Myrna said.

"I know they were interested in my money . . . to an extent," Stephen said. "But I want . . . wanted some happiness in my last years."

"Happiness you would have had with Katharine, may she rest in peace, if your brains hadn't been in the front of your pants," Kate said.

"Ah, what's the use?" Stephen turned away angrily, but Myrna called him back.

"It's all over and done with," she said. "We all love you, let's make this pleasant, after all. . . ."

And once again his sisters began to cry, as did Don, who seemed to be catching their emotions as he would a cold. Finally, Stephen, struck by his own state and circumstances, began to cry.

Prayers were being said beside the grave, and his pallbearers, old friends, stood around the coffin.

"We mustn't be standing here," Cele said. "It's important that *we* be present at the ceremonies," and they all walked over to the grave. It was a good crowd, and Stephen was pleased. Here were friends and family, all gathered to honor him, never mind the mistakes he had made; it was a good showing.

Stephen listened to the prayers, enjoyed the eulogy, although it made him feel more than a little guilty—all that business about taking care of his sons and being a good father. He looked around quickly. Where *were* his sons? John was probably in Europe or something and couldn't make it. Typical. But Martin was there, standing in a clump of relatives, almost hidden by them. He was crying dutifully, although Stephen knew that Martin hated him for what he had done to Katharine.

Not yet ready to face his son, Stephen walked over to his pallbearers. "Hello, Leon," he said to his friend the orthopedic surgeon. "I appreciate you making the trip to be here."

Leon, who wore wire-rim glasses and was dressed in slacks and an open shirt, smiled at him and nodded. Arthur, a retired circuit court judge who was short and bald, also nodded and shook Stephen's hand heartily, as if to indicate that Stephen had indeed done a wonderful thing by dying. "We thought you'd be here," Leon said, "so we flew down. We're going to play some golf and maybe take in a little fishing. We chartered a boat."

"Good," Stephen said, also nodding. "But I think I've had enough of all this already."

"It's almost over," Leon said. "You can at least stay until you're interred, after all, everybody's here."

Stephen did his fatherly duty by walking over to his son and his daughter-in-law and asking how they were. Martin stood stiffly, but then he burst out crying. He finally brought himself under control and said, "I'm sorry, Father. I know I wasn't very understanding, I'm sorry I asked you to stop calling me, but I couldn't stand your constant complaining about Susan and about being alone, not after what you did to Mother."

"I know, I was a bad father," Stephen said, expecting Martin to tell him that, indeed, Stephen had done the best he could and, given all the circumstances, wasn't such a bad father after all. But Martin didn't say anything until Stephen, fighting back his own tears, turned around; and then Martin whispered again, "I'm sorry."

The casket was lowered into the ground. There was the requisite screaming and crying and moaning and rending of garments. At least that's something, Stephen thought. This *is* a good showing.

But suddenly everyone became quiet; it was as if someone had turned off the volume on a television set.

Stephen turned, as did everyone else, to see his old girlfriend Susan walking to the gravesite, big as life and as composed as if she were in her own backyard. She looked ravishing, even though she had recently begun to go to seed: her perfect face had become jowly; the silk dress hugging her hips tightly also accentuated her belly, which was not as flat as it used to be. Her breasts were heavy and her face was made up as if she were going out for cocktails, but still Stephen felt his heart pound in his chest and his breath quicken.

"What the hell are *you* doing here?" Stephen demanded.

Susan placed a bouquet of roses beside the grave and said, "You knew I would be here. I'll always love you."

Stephen heard Leon say something about how she would try to get some money out of Stephen's estate. She did claim her illegitimate child was Stephen's. "You left *me*," Stephen said.

"You wouldn't marry me, after you promised."

"I told you I would take care of you."

"That isn't the same, and you know it. You weren't even man enough to take care of your own child."

Furious, Stephen screamed, "It's not my child. I've always taken care of my family. If you weren't sleeping with every Tom, Dick, and Harry . . ." Mortified at what he had said and how loud he had said it, he looked around at his friends and family. Everyone was watching him with disapproving expressions on their tight faces. They were gloating! Now he had screwed up his own funeral.

There was nothing to do but make the best exit possible under the circumstances. Let Susan enjoy his humiliation. Let them all enjoy it. He would have the last word: he had fixed it so that everything he owned would go to charity, including Susan's condo. He walked through the crowd of relatives and friends and stared straight ahead.

Once inside his car, with the moon roof open and the air-conditioning turned on full blast, he felt better. He drove down the highway and took deep breaths. He had not for a moment looked backward. But he drove aimlessly; he was not ready to return home. There was nothing to watch on television: there were no soaps on Sunday. He couldn't bear the thought of making small talk with anyone. Neither was he hungry, yet he felt a strange emptiness in the pit of his stomach.

Funerals always depress me, he thought. It wasn't Susan; at least *she's* out of my system.

Then he thought about Katharine, all the good years he had had with her, and the guilt rushed back at him. He closed the moon roof; he could think better in the quiet. He remembered carrying Katharine's books from school: she had been his childhood sweetheart. He remembered when she had pawned her wedding ring so he could pay his tuition for law school. He remembered all the tiny apartments, the TV dinners, quarter movies, and nickel egg-creams; and after he had become successful, there were cruises and parties and a succession of spacious houses.

He realized that he truly missed Katharine.

And then it struck him. Why hadn't he thought of it before? He would drive to Brooklyn, where he had been married thirty-five years ago, and attend his own wedding. He would see Katharine. He would go back. . . .

It would be a long drive to Brooklyn, but he had all the time in the world.

nsdale's stories have appeared in The Twilight Zone, *, Creature!, and other magazines and anthologies. He is a Texan who knows exactly what a shadow can't do . . . and what it can do.*

BY THE HAIR OF THE HEAD

by Joe R. Lansdale

The lighthouse was grey and brutally weathered, kissed each morning by a cold, salt spray. Perched there among the rocks and sand, it seemed a last, weak sentinel against an encroaching sea; a relentless, pounding surf that had slowly swallowed up the shoreline and deposited it in the all-consuming belly of the ocean.

Once the lighthouse had been bright-colored, candy-striped like a barber's pole, with a high beacon light and a horn that honked out to the ships on the sea. No more. The lighthouse director, the last of a long line of sea watchers, had cashed in the job ten years back when the need died, but the lighthouse was now his and he lived there alone, bunked down nightly to the tune of the wind and the raging sea.

Below he had renovated the bottom of the tower and built rooms, and one of these he had locked away from all persons, from all eyes but his own.

I came there fresh from college to write my novel, dreams of being the new Norman Mailer dancing in my head. I rented in with him, as he needed a boarder to help him pay for the place, for he no longer worked and his pension was as meager as stale bread.

High up in the top was where we lived, a bamboo partition drawn between our cots each night, giving us some semblance of privacy, and dark curtains were pulled round the thick, foggy windows that traveled the tower completely around.

By day the curtains were drawn and the partition was pulled and I sat at my typewriter, and he, Howard Machen, sat with his book and his pipe, swelled the room full of grey smoke the thickness of his beard. Sometimes he rose and went below, but he was always quiet and never disturbed my work.

It was a pleasant life. Agreeable to both of us. Mornings we had coffee outside on the little railed walkway and had a word or two as well, then I went to my work and he to his book, and at dinner we had food and talk and brandies; sometimes one, sometimes two, depending on mood and the content of our chatter.

We sometimes spoke of the lighthouse and he told me of the old days, of how he had shone that light out many times on the sea. Out like a great, bright fishing line to snag the ships and guide them in; let them follow the light in the manner that Theseus followed Ariadne's thread.

"Was fine," he'd say. "That pretty old light flashing out there. Best job I had in all my born days. Just couldn't leave her when she shut down, so I bought her."

"It is beautiful up here, but lonely at times."

"I have my company."

I took that as a compliment, and we tossed off another brandy. Any idea of my writing later I cast aside. I had done four good pages and was content to spit the rest of the day away in talk and dreams.

"You say this was your best job," I said as a way of conversation. "What did you do before this?"

He lifted his head and looked at me over the briar and its smoke. His eyes squinted against the tinge of the tobacco. "A good many things. I was born in Wales. Moved to Ireland with my family, was brought up there, and went to work there. Learned the carpentry trade from my father. Later I was a tailor. I've also been a mason—note the rooms I built below with my own two hands—and I've been a boat builder and a ventriloquist in a magician's show."

"A ventriloquist?"

"Correct," he said, and his voice danced around me and seemed not to come from where he sat.

"Hey, that's good."

"Not so good really. I was never good, just sort of fell into it. I'm worse now. No practice, but I've no urge to take it up again."

"I've an interest in such things."

"Have you now?"

"Yes."

"Ever tried a bit of voice throwing?"

"No. But it interests me. The magic stuff interests me more. You said you worked in a magician's show?"

"That I did. I was the lead-up act."

"Learn any of the magic tricks, being an insider and all?"

"That I did, but that's not something I'm interested in," he said flatly.

"Was the magician you worked for good?"

"Damn good, m'boy. But his wife was better."

"His wife?"

"Marilyn was her name. A beautiful woman." He winked at me. "Claimed to be a witch."

"You don't say?"

"I do, I do. Said her father was a witch and she learned it and inherited it from him."

"Her father?"

"That's right. Not just women can be witches. Men too."

We poured ourselves another and exchanged sloppy grins, hooked elbows, and tossed it down.

"And another to meet the first," the old man said and poured. Then: "Here's to company." We tossed it off.

"She taught me the ventriloquism, you know," the old man said, relighting his pipe.

"Marilyn?"

"Right, Marilyn."

"She seems to have been a rather all-round lady."

"She was at that. And pretty as an Irish morning."

"I thought witches were all old crones, or young crones. Hook noses, warts . . ."

"Not Marilyn. She was a fine-looking woman. Fine bones, agate eyes that clouded in mystery, and hair the color of a fresh-robbed hive."

"Odd she didn't do the magic herself. I mean, if she was the better magician, why was her husband the star attraction?"

"Oh, but she did do magic. Or rather she helped McDonald to look better than he was, and he was some good. But Marilyn was better.

"Those days were different, m'boy. Women weren't the ones to take the initiative, least not openly. Kept to themselves. Was a sad thing. Back then it wasn't thought fittin' for a woman to be about such business. Wasn't ladylike. Oh, she could get sawed in half, or disappear in a wooden crate, priss and look pretty, but take the lead? Not on your life!"

I fumbled myself another brandy. "A pretty witch, huh?"

"Ummmm."

"Had the old pointed hat and broom passed down, so to speak?" My voice was becoming slightly slurred.

"It's not a laughin' matter, m'boy." Machen clenched the pipe in his teeth.

"I've touched a nerve, have I not? I apologize. Too much sauce."

Machen smiled. "Not at all. It's a silly thing, you're right. To hell with it."

"No, no, I'm the one who spoiled the fun. You were telling me she claimed to be the descendant of a long line of witches."

Machen smiled. It did not remind me of other smiles he had worn. This one seemed to come from a borrowed collection.

"Just some silly tattle is all. Don't really know much about it, just worked for her, m'boy." That was the end of that. Standing, he knocked out his pipe on the concrete floor and went to his cot.

For moment I sat there, the last breath of Machen's pipe still in the air, the brandy still warm in my throat and stomach. I looked at the windows that surrounded the lighthouse, and everywhere I looked was my own ghostly reflection. It was like looking out through the compound eyes of an insect, seeing a multiple image.

I turned out the lights, pulled the curtains and drew the partition between our beds, wrapped myself in my blanket, and soon washed up on the distant shore of a recurring dream. A dream not quite in grasp, but heard like the far, fuzzy cry of a gull out from land.

It had been with me almost since moving into the tower. Sounds, voices . . .

A clunking noise like peg legs on stone. . . .

. . . a voice, fading in, fading out . . . Machen's voice, the words not quite clear, but soft and coaxing . . . then solid and firm: "Then be a beast. Have your own way. Look away from me with your mother's eyes."

". . . your fault," came a child's voice, followed by other words that were chopped out by the howl of the sea wind, the roar of the waves.

". . . getting too loud. He'll hear . . ." came Machen's voice.

"Don't care . . . I . . . ," lost voices now.

I tried to stir, but then the tube of sleep, nourished by the brandy, came unclogged, and I descended down into richer blackness.

Was a bright morning full of sun, and no fog for a change. Cool clear out there on the landing, and the sea even seemed to roll in soft and bounce against the rocks and lighthouse like puffy cotton balls blown on the wind.

I was out there with my morning coffee, holding the cup in one hand and grasping the railing with the other. It was a narrow area but safe enough, provided you didn't lean too far out or run along the walk when it was slick with rain. Machen told me of a man who had done just that and found himself plummeting over to be shattered like a dropped melon on the rocks below.

Machen came out with a cup of coffee in one hand, his unlit pipe in the other. He looked haggard this morning, as if a bit of old age had crept upon him in the night, fastened a straw to his face, and sucked out part of his substance.

"Morning," I said.

"Morning." He emptied his cup in one long draft. He balanced the cup on the metal railing and began to pack his pipe.

"Sleep bad?" I asked.

He looked at me, then at his pipe, finished his packing, and put the pouch away in his coat pocket. He took a long match from the same pocket, gave it fire with his thumbnail, lit the pipe. He puffed quite awhile before he answered me. "Not too well. Not too well."

"We drank too much."

"We did at that."

I sipped my coffee and looked at the sky, watched a snowy gull dive down and peck at the foam, rise up with a wriggling fish in its beak. It climbed high in the sky, became a speck of froth on crystal blue.

"I had funny dreams," I said. "I think I've had them all along, since I came here. But last night they were stronger than ever."

"Oh?"

"Thought I heard your voice speaking to someone. Thought I heard steps on the stairs, or more like the plunking of peg legs, like those old sea captains have."

"You don't say?"

"And another voice, a child's."

"That right? Well . . . maybe you did hear me speakin'. I wasn't entirely straight with you last night. I do have quite an interest in the voice throwing, and I practice it from time to time on my dummy. Last night must have been louder than usual, being drunk and all."

"Dummy?"

"My old dummy from the act. Keep it in the room below."

"Could I see it?"

He grimaced. "Maybe another time. It's kind of a private thing with me. Only bring her out when we're alone."

"Her?"

"Right. Name's Caroline, a right smart-looking girl dummy, rosy cheeked with blonde pigtails."

"Well, maybe someday I can look at her."

"Maybe someday." He stood up, popped the contents of the pipe out over the railing, and started inside. Then he turned: "I talk too much. Pay no mind to an old, crazy man."

Then he was gone, and I was there with a hot cup of coffee, a bright, warm day, and an odd, unexplained chill at the base of my bones.

Two days later we got on witches again, and I guess it was my fault. We hit the brandy hard that night. I had sold a short story for a goodly sum—my largest check to date—and we were celebrating and talking and saying how my fame would be as high as the stars. We got pretty sicky there, and to hear Machen tell it, and to hear me agree—no matter he hadn't read the story—I was another Hemingway, Wolfe, and Fitzgerald all balled into one.

"If Marilyn were here," I said thoughtlessly, drunk, "why we could get her to consult her crystal and tell us my literary future."

"Why that's nonsense, she used no crystal."

"No crystal, broom, or pointed hat? No eerie evil deeds for her? A white magician no doubt?"

"Magic is magic, m'boy. And even good intentions can backfire."

"Whatever happened to her, Marilyn I mean?"

"Dead."

"Old age?"

"Died young and beautiful, m'boy. Grief killed her."

"I see," I said, as you'll do to show attentiveness.

Suddenly, it was as if the memories were a balloon overloaded with air, about to burst if pressure were not taken off. So, he let loose the pressure and began to talk.

"She took her a lover, Marilyn did. Taught him many a thing, about love, magic, what have you. Lost her husband on account of it, the magician, I mean. Lost respect for herself in time.

"You see, there was this little girl she had, by her lover. A fine-looking sprite, lived until she was three. Had no proper father. He had taken to the sea and had never much entertained the idea of marryin' Marilyn. Keep them stringing was his motto then, damn his eyes. So he left them to fend for themselves."

"What happened to the child?"

"She died. Some childhood disease."

"That's sad," I said, "a little girl gone and having only sipped at life."

"Gone? Oh no. There's the soul, you know."

I wasn't much of a believer in the soul and I said so.

"Oh, but there is a soul. The body perishes but the soul lives on."

"I've seen no evidence of it."

"But I have," Machen said solemnly. "Marilyn was determined that the girl would live on, if not in her own form, then in another."

"Hogwash!"

Machen looked at me sternly. "Maybe. You see, there is a part of witchcraft that deals with the soul, a part that believes the soul can be trapped and held, kept from escaping this earth and into the beyond. That's why a lot of natives are superstitious about having their picture taken. They believe once their image is captured, through magic, their soul can be contained.

"Voodoo works much the same. It's nothing but another form of witchcraft. Practitioners of that art believe their souls can be held to this earth by means of someone collecting nail parin's or hair from them while they're still alive.

"That's what Marilyn had in mind. When she saw the girl was fadin', she snipped one of the girl's long pigtails and kept it to herself. Cast spells on it while the child lay dyin', and again after life had left the child."

"The soul was supposed to be contained within the hair?"

"That's right. It can be restored, in a sense, to some other object through the hair. It's like those voodoo dolls. A bit of hair or nail parin' is collected from the person you want to control, or if not control, maintain the presence of their soul, and it's sewn into those dolls. That way, when the pins are stuck into the doll, the living suffer, and when they die their soul is trapped in the doll for all eternity, or rather as long as the doll with its hair or nail parin's exists."

"So she preserved the hair so she could make a doll and have the little girl live on, in a sense?"

"Something like that."

"Sounds crazy."

"I suppose."

"And what of the little girl's father?"

"Ah, that sonofabitch! He came home to find the little girl dead and buried and the mother mad. But there was that little gold lock of hair, and knowing Marilyn, he figured her intentions."

"Machen," I said slowly. "It was you, was it not? You were the father?"

"I was."

"I'm sorry."

"Don't be. We were both foolish. I was the more foolish. She left her husband for me and I cast her aside. Ignored my own child. I was the fool, a great fool."

"Do you really believe in that stuff about the soul? About the hair and what Marilyn was doing?"

"Better I didn't. A soul once lost from the body would best

prefer to be departed I think . . . but love is sometimes a brutal thing."

We just sat there after that. We drank more. Machen smoked his pipe, and about an hour later we went to bed.

There were sounds again, gnawing at the edge of my sleep. The sounds that had always been there, but now, since we had talked of Marilyn, I was less able to drift off into blissful slumber. I kept thinking of those crazy things Machen had said. I remembered, too, those voices I had heard, and the fact that Machen was a ventriloquist, and perhaps, not altogether stable.

But those sounds.

I sat up and opened my eyes. They were coming from below. Voices. Machen's first. ". . . not be the death of you, girl, not at all . . . my only reminder of Marilyn . . ."

And then to my horror. "Let me be, Papa. Let it end." The last had been a little girl's voice, but the words had been bitter and wise beyond the youngness of tone.

I stepped out of bed and into my trousers, crept to the curtain, and looked on Machen's side.

Nothing, just a lonely cot. I wasn't dreaming. I had heard him all right, and the other voice . . . it had to be that Machen, grieved over what he had done in the past, over Marilyn's death, had taken to speaking to himself in the little girl's voice. All that stuff Marilyn had told him about the soul, it had gotten to him, cracked his stability.

I climbed down the cold metal stairs, listening. Below I heard the old, weathered door that led outside slam. Heard the thud of boots going down the outside steps.

I went back up, went to the windows, and pulling back the curtains section by section, finally saw the old man. He was carrying something wrapped in a black cloth and he had a shovel in his hand. I watched as, out there by the shore, he dug a shallow grave and placed the cloth-wrapped object within, placed a rock over it, and left it to the night and the incoming tide.

I pretended to be asleep when he returned, and later, when I felt certain he was well visited by Morpheus, I went downstairs and retrieved the shovel from the tool room. I went out to where I had seen him dig and went to work, first turning over the large

stone and shoveling down into the pebbly dirt. Due to the fresh-
ness of the hole, it was easy digging.

I found the cloth and what was inside. It made me flinch at first,
it looked so real. I thought it was a little rosy-cheeked girl buried
alive, for it looked alive . . . but it was a dummy. A ventriloquist
dummy. It had aged badly, as if water had gotten to it. In some
ways it looked as if it were rotting from the inside out. My finger
went easily and deeply into the wood of one of the legs.

Out of some odd curiosity, I reached up and pushed back the
wooden eyelids. There were no wooden painted eyes, just darkness, empty sockets that uncomfortably reminded me of looking
down into the black hollows of a human skull. And the hair. On
one side of the head was a yellow pigtail, but where the other
should have been was a bare spot, as if the hair had been ripped
away from the wooden skull.

With a trembling hand I closed the lids down over those empty
eyes, put the dirt back in place, the rock, and returned to bed.
But I did not sleep well. I dreamed of a grown man talking to a
wooden doll and using another voice to answer back, pretending
that the doll lived and loved him too.

But the water had gotten to it, and the sight of those rotting
legs had snapped him back to reality, dashed his insane hopes of
containing a soul by magic, shocked him brutally from foolish
dreams. Dead is dead.

The next day, Machen was silent and had little to say. I suspected the events of last night weighed on his mind. Our conversation must have returned to him this morning in sober memory,
and he, somewhat embarrassed, was reluctant to recall it. He
kept to himself down below in the locked room, and I busied
myself with my work.

It was night when he came up, and there was a smug look
about him, as if he had accomplished some great deed. We spoke
a bit, but not of witches, of past times and the sea. Then he pulled
back the curtains and looked at the moon rise above the water
like a cold fish eye.

"Machen," I said, "maybe I shouldn't say anything, but if you
should ever have something bothering you. If you should ever
want to talk about it . . . Well, feel free to come to me."

He smiled at me. "Thank you. But any problem that might have been bothering me is . . . shall we say, all sewn up."

We said little more and soon went to bed.

I slept sounder that night, but again I was rousted from my dreams by voices. Machen's voice again, and then the poor man speaking in that little child's voice.

"It's a fine home for you," Machen said in his own voice.

"I want no home," came the little girl's voice. "I want to be free."

"You want to stay with me, with the living. You're just not thinking. There's only darkness beyond the veil."

The voices were very clear and loud. I sat up in bed and strained my ears.

"It's where I belong," the little girl's voice again, but it spoke not in a little girl manner. There was only the tone.

"Things have been bad lately," Machen said. "And you're not yourself."

Laughter, horrible little girl laughter.

"I haven't been myself for years."

"Now, Catherine . . . play your piano. You used to play it so well. Why, you haven't touched it in years."

"Play. Play. With these!"

"You're too loud."

"I don't care. Let him hear, let him . . ."

A door closed sharply and the sound died off to a mumble, a word caught here and there was scattered and confused by the throb of the sea.

Next morning Machen had nothing for me, not even a smile from his borrowed collection. Nothing but coldness, his back, and a frown.

I saw little of him after coffee, and once, from below—for he stayed down there the whole day through—I thought I heard him cry in a loud voice, "Have it your way then," and then there was the sound of a slamming door and some other sort of commotion below.

After a while I looked out at the land and the sea, and down there, striding back and forth, hands behind his back, went

Machen, like some great confused penguin contemplating the far shore.

I like to think there was something more than curiosity in what I did next. Like to think I was looking for the source of my friend's agony; looking for some way to help him find peace.

I went downstairs and pulled at the door he kept locked, hoping that, in his anguish, he had forgotten to lock it back. He had not forgotten.

I pressed my ear against the door and listened. Was that crying I heard?

No. I was being susceptible, caught up in Machen's fantasy. It was merely the wind whipping about the tower.

I went back upstairs, had coffee, and wrote not a line.

So day fell into night, and I could not sleep but finally got the strange business out of my mind by reading a novel. A rollicking good sea story of daring men and bloody battles, great ships clashing in a merciless sea.

And then, from his side of the curtain, I heard Machen creak off his cot and take to the stairs. One flight below was the door that led to the railing round about the tower, and I heard that open and close.

I rose, folded a small piece of paper into my book for a marker, and pulled back one of the window curtains. I walked around pulling curtains and looking until I could see him below.

He stood with his hands behind his back, looking out at the sea like a stern father keeping an eye on his children. Then, calmly, he mounted the railing and leaped out into the air.

I ran. Not that it mattered, but I ran, out to the railing . . . and looked down. His body looked like a rag doll splayed on the rocks.

There was no question in my mind that he was dead, but slowly I wound my way down the steps . . . and was distracted by the room. The door stood wide open.

I don't know what compelled me to look in, but I was drawn to it. It was a small room with a desk and a lot of shelves filled with books, mostly occult and black magic. There were carpentry tools on the wall, and all manner of needles and devices that might be used by a tailor. The air was filled with an odd odor I could not place, and on Machen's desk, something that was definitely not tobacco smoldered away.

There was another room beyond the one in which I stood. The door to it was cracked open. I pushed it back and stepped inside. It was a little child's room filled thick with toys and such: jack-in-the-boxes, dolls, kid books, and a toy piano. All were covered in dust.

On the bed lay a teddy bear. It was ripped open and the stuffing was pulled out. There was one long strand of hair hanging out of that gutted belly, just one, as if it were the last morsel of a greater whole. It was the color of honey from a fresh-robbed hive. I knew what the smell in the ashtray was now.

I took the hair and put a match to it, just in case.

Dreams, supposedly, are the method by which our subconscious works out our day-to-day emotional and psychological problems in symbolic fashion, enabling us thereby to cope with the so-called real world. Nightmares are dreams. The real world has often been described as a nightmare. Nightmares aren't always populated with horrible creatures. The real world . . .

Elisabeth Erica Burden is a Texan, mother, and a writer of no small potential. This is her first sale.

DREAMS

by Elisabeth Erica Burden

The clock chimes once, perhaps only sounding the half hour within all hours. By my bed I gather into darkness, then step forth, a shadow, into the moonlight of another time.

I enter the house, not by any of the doors; I stand in the study, in the middle of the room. Heavy drapes frame tall, narrow windows. The great mahogany desk stands at an angle; a square marble block presses down the pages of an open ledger, and the winter moon pours light over the globe of the world.

In the living room, moonlight touches the wood of the piano, lies on the couch of blue velvet, and forms pools of silver on the console with its top of glass. And across the room, between the windows, a long, pale face drifts from dark oils framed in brownish gold.

I enter the high, spacious hall. The mirror by the heavy front door has caught a moonbeam and holds it. In the glass the angles of the walls converge behind me, unobstructed by my presence. I pass the little tables that are pushed against the wall, stop and peer up into the blackness of the staircase that curves to the long narrow hall above.

In my bed I lie, immovable, bound by the web of dreams. I focus my eyes behind my lids and see myself ascend, merge into the darkness that floats from the curving stairs.

I am by the window in the hall upstairs. The wind has come to life and sweeps the branches of the elm tree across the roof of the porch below. I walk down the hall, follow the patterns of drifting light and shadow. There are two doors on the right, one on the left; all are closed. I turn the corner and stop before the small room that used to be the nursery. The white door shines dimly out of darkness. There is a brass handle, not a knob; my hand reaches for it, holds it, slowly presses it down.

I strain against the iron net of sleep that holds me, strive to free my lids from heaviness. *Don't!* I want to scream. *Don't open this door!*

I am a shadow, untouched by light. The handle moves down; the door opens slowly.

But now I wrestle with sleep, twist, turn, heave, and, finally, break out of bondage, break the spell for the third time in as many nights. But though I sit up and my eyes are open, I am caught in the warped time of dreaming for just a moment longer: I still hold the handle of the door. Then, suddenly, my dream-self, dark and blurred, disintegrating, enters my dimension of wakefulness and collides with me.

I switch on the light, throw off the covers. I look into the bathroom mirror and stare at myself. The skin underneath my eyes is blue, translucent, and my lips are nearly white.

In my small kitchen, dirty dishes are stacked in the sink, and roaches scatter across the countertops. I rinse a glass and heat some milk. I put my head on the table, stretch out my arm, feel the glass warm in my hand.

For almost two decades now, my childhood was imprisoned: I live unhaunted by memories. Right after my mother was murdered, when I was barely fifteen, I locked away everything that came before. Within myself there was great silence; I never asked Aunt Valerie, and she kept quiet, too.

When I raise my head again, I feel myself grow cold. A strange transformation is taking place: the past superimposes itself on the present. A soft oval curves smoothly within the straight lines of my kitchen table, and a transparent, checkered linen cloth floats inside hard formica. My father sits across from me; through him I see my window and, beyond, in the darkness of the night, the stove with the large, gleaming copper kettle and all the shining pots and pans on their hooks. I see through my refrigerator; behind it is the open door of the pantry.

My father becomes solid now, leans toward me. He takes my hand into both of his and holds it so tightly that I want to take it back and shake away the pain. I am fourteen, and I hear his words but do not understand their meaning.

I withdraw my hand. All becomes transparent again, and he fades into the darkness that presses against my kitchen window. With him the stove, kettle, pots, and pans float off. The refrigerator has begun to hum; the pantry is gone. There is blood running down my arm. The glass is crushed; sharp, jagged pieces press into my palm. My blood joins rivulets of milk on the table and trickles, warm, into my lap.

The dreams have forged cracks in the walls of the prison; memories have begun to escape.

By the sink, I hold up my hand and scream.

Morning disappears in misty rain. Streets, cars, people are grey, indistinguishable from one another. On the bus the air is humid, steaming with the dampness of coats, hats, mufflers. The woman next to me leans forward, takes off her cap, frees her hair. I see her reflection in the window, and I see my own face, pale, distorted, dark holes where my eyes should be. Outside, streets pass by, grey houses, barren trees. But riding with me now, in the window glass, is the reflection of the kitchen: wrought-iron light fixtures, the stove with the copper kettle, the pantry.

I am rinsing dishes. It is dark outside; in the window above the sink I see my own reflection. With wet hands I push away strands of tangled hair. Behind me the kitchen door opens. I see my mother enter, remove her hat. Her hair falls to her shoulders, dark and curly; her cheeks are flushed from the cold. She looks at me but does not know that I am watching her, too.

Then, for a moment, I am confused. The face of a stranger blocks her reflection, blots out the kitchen. The woman next to me gets up and pulls the cord. The bus comes to a hard stop. Small drops of rain fall against the window, disintegrate.

When we pull away from the curb, night comes again; my mother is back. She stands by the pantry, frowns, takes off her coat, and walks toward the dining room. Now my father comes in, looking angry. He passes behind me, reaches for my mother. He speaks to her; she shrugs. Suddenly, he takes her arm, shakes

her, shouts. I turn off the water and turn around. Both look at me;
he lets go of her. She straightens and smoothes the sleeve of her
soft lavender blouse.

"Julie," she says, "you've been an awful long time doing these
few dishes." She glances at me from the door to the dining room.
"And, Julie, look at you! You're nearly twelve, and you still don't
know how to comb your hair."

My father comes toward me and gently touches my cheek.

"Ma'am, did you want to get off here? This is the end of the
line." The driver is leaning over me. The bus is empty.

Virginia Hagerty looks up from her desk when I enter the
library.

"Sorry, I'm late," I murmur.

"You look pale." She sees the bandage. "What happened to
your hand?"

Claire Fields is already working on the catalogues. I hurry past
her. She looks at me and frowns.

Night comes early. I sit at my table and eat the soup I heated
right from the pan. Shadows come out of corners, creep toward
me. I flip on the light, drive them back into hiding. The naked
bulb glares at me from the ceiling—a small, angry sun burns
above my head. I squint, let my eyes adjust to the sudden brightness, see the walls of the kitchen become transparent and recede
into pastures, smell honeysuckle and wild roses. The sun becomes large, hot, is high above the house and paints patterns of
leaves on the porch. My cat, Emmanuel, gets up and stretches,
rubs against one of the thick columns, and comes away with
flakes of paint on his yellow coat.

I am hiding underneath the stairs, look up through the cracks.
The screen door slams, heavy boots cross the porch, come down
above my head, walk across the gravel. I wait until I hear the
engine start, then climb up on the porch.

My mother comes down the curving staircase. She carries a
tray with a bottle and glasses. I watch her walk into the living
room. I enter the house, hold onto the screen, and let it close
quietly.

She stops, looks around. "Where've you been? I waited all morning for you to come home."

I remain silent, pick thorns from my arms and legs, know that if I hadn't gotten a ride back from Embleton, I'd still be walking up the road.

"You mailed my letter?"

I nod and follow her into the kitchen. She puts away the bottle, rinses the glasses, turns and kicks Emmanuel, who had come too close.

I look down, study the straps of my sandals, watch my toes spread out and wiggle.

"Never mind!" She turns away from me. "But it wouldn't do to tell your father that Mr. Brooks was here. You know how your father hates him, though I don't, for the life of me, know why."

I am only ten, but I know why my father hates Mr. Brooks. And I know why he is beginning to hate my mother, too.

The light bulb dies suddenly. Startled, I knock the saucepan off the table, get up in the dark and feel the remains of the soup, thick, coagulated, underneath the soles of my feet.

In the living room I sit on the old, sagging couch. I hear the hum of the refrigerator from the kitchen; then all is quiet.

But they are talking in the study. I am hiding in the thick cushions of the blue velvet couch. The pale face in the painting is turned toward me; dark eyes stare in the dim light.

"Jesus Christ, Suzanne!" My father's voice, disembodied, comes toward me. "How can you run up another bill when most of the land is up for sale already and we have to take out another mortgage on the house?"

Yellow light pours from the open door of the study, and my mother's shadow, vast and sharp, moves across the wall. Her head is creased by the angle of wall and ceiling; huge fingers spread out above me, then retract into a fist.

"Is it my fault," she shouts, "that you can't make a decent living?"

Emmanuel jumps up on me, and I, scared, race out into the hall and up the stairs.

Coming home from the library, the buses, crowded, pass me by. Tucking the ends of my muffler into my coat, pulling my cap

over my ears, I begin to walk and take the shortcut through the
park. Suddenly, out of the mists that float above the damp earth,
an old woman comes to me. Her black coat is heavy and hides the
tops of her boots. A black scarf covers her hair and is tied underneath her chin. She comes close and peers into my face. I draw
back, uneasy, wondering.

"I mean no harm," she mutters. "Excuse my interference."

She takes hold of my sleeve and draws me toward the pale
circle of light underneath the street lamp. I try to break away,
but the grip on my arm tightens.

"Be still!" she says. "Don't be afraid!"

She takes my hand, studies my palm, and frowns. "Such as
this," she says, "I haven't seen in years."

"What is it?" I cry. "What do you see? What's happening to
me?"

She looks at me and smiles, her face a net of deep wrinkles, her
gums toothless, smooth and brown. "Who can say just yet? Give it
more time."

I stand by the lamp and see her, small and dark and bent, walk
back up the path and step into the shadows of the coming night.

"Who are you?" I call after her. "What do you want of me?"

"It's you who needs me," she calls back. "It's you who'll be
wanting things of me."

In my apartment I count the hours. When midnight comes I
get my coat, slip on my boots and, afraid of waking, afraid of
sleeping, go out into the streets.

Light rain is falling. Everything is deserted, quiet. I turn the
corner, and, suddenly, the dark silent houses, the whole street,
rise up at an angle, speed off toward a point in the far horizon,
become smaller and smaller, are sucked into it, are gone.

Before me is the lane that winds down the hill from the back of
the house. Fields stretch around me, shrouded white in winter
death. My father is coming up the lane, walking toward me. I
remember that he had been trying to tell me something the
night before, still feel the pain in my hand that he had held so
tight.

"Mother thought you went to Winona to find a buyer for the
house. She didn't expect you back before tonight."

He is silent. His face is white, and snow lies white on his hair.

"Don't go home now!" I cry, suddenly remembering my mother's trunks and bags out in the hall and the car that waited in the driveway.

He bends over me stiffly, touches my forehead with cold lips, then walks past me.

"Don't go, Father!" I jump back into the middle of the lane, barring his path.

Brakes screech. Snow-covered fields vanish into darkness. Two men are looking out from a car.

"Are you all right, ma'am?" The one nearest me gets out, and I see the uniform and the plastic domes on the rack that is mounted to the roof of the car.

"Are you all right? Do you need a ride home?"

I swallow, clear my throat, force myself to speak. "Thank you, Officer," I murmur.

He studies me.

"Very kind of you." I speak louder now. "Thank you. But I couldn't sleep. Thought I'd walk around a bit."

"We'll take you home."

"So kind. But I live right around the corner."

I turn, walk away slowly. Behind me the men are talking, then I hear the car door slam.

In my bed sleep comes and wraps itself around me.

The moon shines into the study; circles of muted light lie on the piano in the living room. Dark eyes follow me from the pale face that hangs between the windows. I enter the hall, merge into the darkness of the stairs, stand by the window. Branches of the elm tree knock on the roof of the porch below. Patches of light dance across shadows in the long, narrow hall. I turn the corner, stop before the white door, press down the handle.

Again, I fight to break the spell.

The door opens into the nursery. The bed and cedar wardrobe are in shadows; the small table is pushed against the opposite wall. The matching chair lies on its back in the middle. Above it, two black shoes hang in the air. Dark trousers merge up into darkness. Hands, hanging loose and open, form patches of white against the dark of the legs. The torso is invisible, but from below the ceiling a pale oval gleams at me.

I reach for the light switch. Brightness bursts into the room. There are stuffed animals on shelves in the corners, looking at me with round, glassy eyes. A mouse jumps out from underneath the chair, runs across the bare wood of the floor. From high above, my father looks at me. A strand of dark hair lies in the middle of the forehead, forms a peak, a point, right above his nose. His eyes, huge and round, protrude from their sockets, have sprung halfway from his head. And his tongue is almost black and broad and thick; it fills his mouth, covers his lips, and lies heavy on his chin.

It is nearly noon before I call the library.

"We were worried about you, Julie." Virginia Hagerty's voice comes from the receiver. "We thought you might need a rest. You haven't been yourself lately, you know." There is a pause, then she speaks again. "Well, sure hope you'll be feeling better. Let us know if you need anything."

I stay in bed the whole day and look at cracks in the ceiling. It is early evening before I dress and go out to buy food.

The supermarket is crowded; people jostle me. I reach for a can of soup, stretch toward the upper shelf. Some women have gathered in the next aisle; I hear them but don't know what they say.

When I turn, the aisles become shorter and narrow; the whole store shrinks. White letters form an arc on the window: Pearson's Grocery, spelled backward looking out. I stand in the corner by bags of meal and flour and check the list my mother made. To the left of me, hidden by shelves, people are talking, their words punctuated by the ring of the cash register up front.

"What a shame!" The woman's voice is shrill and high. "And him always so nice. He did it because of her, of course."

"Shush," comes the voice of another woman.

"But it's true!" The first one continues. "Everybody knows how she treated him. All the different men she carried on with, right under his nose. I always thought it'd be her that comes to a bad end. If you ask me, she married him for his money; that's all she ever wanted from him."

"Well, if that's what she wanted, she got all he had." A man is speaking now. "He used to be one of the richest men in the county, but he had to sell his land piece by piece. Heard he was ready to sell the house too, right before he hung himself."

I am caught in the trap of their conversation, don't want to listen but must hear. Then I pull myself together, jump out from the dimness of the corner, run toward the light coming from the open door. In passing, I see their faces, now full of surprise.

"Good Lord! Wasn't that . . . ?" I hear one of them say.

"Ma'am! Ma'am!" the boy shouts after me as I run out of the supermarket, clutching the basket with food. He catches up with me. "The checkout, ma'am," he says, "is over there."

The cracks in the ceiling slant and curl. My telephone begins to ring, and I lie still and count the rings. Now, there are heavy footsteps on the stairs. I get up slowly and open the door just a little bit.

The long narrow hall is dimly lit. A man, a stranger, walks up the curving stairs. He is tall and broad and red-faced, wears a checkered shirt and a cowboy hat. He comes down the hall now, hitches up his jeans, and steps down heavy with his high-heeled boots.

"Shhh!" My mother is behind him and puts a finger to her lips.

But then she sees the light from my door, comes toward it, kicks it open, raises her hand, and slaps my face. The man turns around, looks at me, and grins.

"You sneak!" she yells and pulls on my hair. "There you are again, spying on me, just like you always did. I tell you, if it weren't for your spying, your father'd be still alive today!"

All is dark and quiet now. Sleep takes me. I try to fight it, wrestle with it.

I pass through the living room. Shadows flicker over the face in the painting. The moon, incomplete, not quite full, races across a black, stormy sky. Upstairs I stop by the window; the wind comes and rattles its panes. Patches of light are driven before me, flicker, and die. There are two doors on the right, one on the left. I stand by the single door and listen, then take the handle and slowly press it down.

Two windows break the wall on the other side of the room. White, sheer curtains shroud the glass. Beyond them, the tops of trees sway in the wind. For a moment the room lies in darkness; the moon had disappeared from the sky. Then, again, light flickers across the walls, the ceiling, and the floor. I look into the mirror across from me: the door behind me closes softly, its whole length, uninterrupted, captured in the glass. I walk toward the bed; above it, slender trunks of birch trees gleam inside a silver frame.

My mother's face is turned toward me. Her lids are closed. The mouth is partly open, and she breathes deep and evenly. She moves an arm and lets it slide down by her side. Slowly, I put my knee on the bed, careful not to wake her. I reach across her, take a pillow, but she stirs, and I draw back. She moans, is quiet, lies still again, and, again, I take the pillow and hold it right above her head.

From my own bed, I watch. The images are blurred now, distorted, and move across my lids like slow-motion film.

Underneath me, her body rises slowly, lifts me high into the air, descends toward the bed, and arches up again. Coming down, her arms lift slowly, move toward my head, and leave behind them, again and again, images of themselves where empty space should have been. A dozen pale arms and hands fan out from the covers, draw all back into the ones that have found my hair. One foot frees itself from tangled sheets, strains toward the board. The heel now touches wood, sets off slowly widening circles of light that spread and dissolve into a dull thud that echoes, over and over, inside my head.

And, slowly, she bucks and thrashes, lifts me up, holds me there, and brings me down again. Her hands clutch my hair; my head goes forward, forever following her. Then I begin to slide, float onto the bed, bounce off the covers, and see the pillow slipping from her face. But now my father's head drifts from the ceiling, turns on its axis, floats down to me through light and shadows, and comes to rest between my hands. I hold it tightly until, at last, she stops her moving. With her dark hair spread across white pillows, she lies still in her bed.

Outside, the moon is racing through storm clouds. But I fly

down the stairs and into the study, slide up the walls and across the ceiling, and flit back and forth through the room.

I sit up in my bed, awake. I hear my own shadow's screams come to me from the past, and I reach out toward it and stop its racing and pull it back to me again.

I get up and look into my eyes in the mirror and read the truth in my face. Now I remember everything; I even remember how I forgot:

On that day, a thunderstorm was raging. I sat on the blue velvet couch. My Aunt Valerie had her arms around me, and I, in turn, held Emmanuel. Down by the pond, lightning struck a willow. Cars filled the driveway; strangers were all over the house.

A man paced up and down by the fireplace, walked toward the windows, studied the painting, and turned to me again.

"But when you called your aunt this morning," he said, "you told her that you had *seen* the man."

I stroked Emmanuel.

"And you can't give us a description? Don't even remember what he looked like? You saw him coming up the stairs. Was he tall? Was he short? What was he wearing?"

"No! No! No!" I cried suddenly. Emmanuel jumped from my lap, and Aunt Valerie drew me closer. "I don't remember! Leave me alone!"

"He had dark hair," the man said. "Kind of like yours. Right?"

"No! No! No!" I held both hands to my head and tried to cover my hair.

"Leave her alone for now," said Aunt Valerie. "The child just lost her mother. Good Lord, man! Can't you be more gentle with her?"

A woman came in from the study, sat down beside me, and took my hands. "Don't you want to see him get caught? Pay for what he did?"

"No! No! No!" I cried. "I don't remember! Leave me alone!"

Boots came down the stairs; another man came in.

"Sir," he said, "I bet we can start looking for somebody bald. She had a ton of hair in her hands." He laughed by sucking air into his throat and sounded like somebody choking. He looked at me and stopped, but my whimpers had already turned into a wail so shrill and so high that the couch began to spin. The room was rotating, corner over corner, and the painting on the wall whirled around so fast that the face became a glowing coil.

When, finally, all motion stopped, I only vaguely remembered that something terrible had happened and that my Aunt Valerie was here to take me away.

When dusk comes, I dress and go to the park to wait for the old woman, for now I know what she meant when she said that I would be needing her. With night, soft rain begins to fall, and I cling to the streetlight and begin to call for her.

She steps out of darkness into the dim circle of light and peers up into my face. "It's still too soon." She shakes her head. "It hasn't happened yet."

"Too soon?" I whisper. "The dreams. The memories . . ."

"You walk in your dreams?"

"I walk, but not even the mirrors show that I'm there."

"But your dreams are still dreams of the past?"

I nod. "The memories," I say. "Things of the past."

She cuts me short. "It's too soon." The wind blows the ends of her scarf into her face, and she tucks them into her coat. "It's still too soon, but when it happens, I'll help you, and, in return for the favor, you bring me a soul."

"A soul?" I asked, not sure that I have heard her right.

She laughs. "When it happens, I'll help you, but I need a soul."

"What are you saying?" I draw back from her, step out of the light. "When what happens? And what is this about a soul?"

"Questions, questions," she mutters and steps forward, comes close to me again. "You'll know soon enough. And you bring me a soul."

"A soul!" I try to see her in the night. "Mine?"

She laughs again. "Not yours. Yours is not for the giving or for the taking. Yours has long been spoken for."

Rain and wind come through the night and knock on my window. Sleep enters and holds me tight.

In the study, the moon pours cold light over the globe of the world. I pass into the living room, move toward the long, pale face. But, suddenly, gusts of wind rise from the corners, sweep toward me, lift me, twist me, tear me apart and scatter my fragments. Then all is still, and, slowly, I drift together again. The walls become luminous, bend inward; the angles converge on me. Then all shifts back, settles into familiar dimensions. I stand under bright lights.

In the center of the room, near me, is a sofa. Brown flowers wilt on its rumpled, dark-green cover, from which the fringes hang ragged or are gone. The coffeetable holds dirty plates and ashtrays. Crushed beer cans litter the floor. Between the two windows is the print of a landscape; around it, the wallpaper hangs in shreds. And where the piano used to be is a huge television set. Blobs and blurs of color run across its silent screen.

I turn my head and now see the two people who sit and face the television. The man has thrown out a leg and folded his hands across his stomach. His head hangs down; his chin rests on his chest. The woman is curled up in her chair. She shakes a bottle of bright-red polish and paints her fingernails.

"Wake up, I tell ya!" she says to the man. "The damn box's on the blink again."

The man raises his head, stretches, is just about to say something, then he sees me and stares. The woman looks at him, then turns and looks in my direction. Her blue-rimmed eyes bulge slightly; her hands grip the chair. The man has raised himself halfway and supports himself and thick arms from which cords of muscles have sprung. Time is suspended, the moment captured in a single, motionless frame.

From my bed, I see myself stand frozen, and I see them, being just as still.

I look around: the room holds me inside itself like a magnet, and I don't know how to get out. I take a few steps back and pass through the sofa and table and stop with my hip and leg inside the television set. The woman is standing now; the man had dropped back into his chair. I run toward the far wall, and, finally, both of them scream. I race over the walls and ceiling in panic, and when I come near them the woman faints, falls limply to the floor, and the man runs out into the hall and throws himself against the warped, creaking door.

The phone rings early in the morning; Virginia Hagerty wants to know how I feel. In the afternoon Claire Fields brings me cheesecake, makes the coffee, glances at the dirty dishes, all the things that have fallen to the floor. But in the evening, at the twilight hour, I put on my coat and boots.

The wind is tugging on my muffler, whips the ends into my face, wraps my coat around my legs and drives patches of mist into the ground.

"Has it happened, then?" The old woman looks up into my face.

"Last night," I say. "It all began as usual, but then . . ."

"The dream turned into a haunting. Here!" She takes her hand from her pocket. "This is what I brought for you."

On a small silver chain a pale, green stone, a teardrop, gathers a faint halo of light. I look at her, silent, wait for an explanation.

"Wear it around your neck. Touch it. It'll wake you and bring you back."

I take the stone, look at it, then slip it into my bag. "How much do you want for it?" I ask.

"How much!" she says. "How much! It's not how much but what!"

"What do you want for it, then?"

"Have you forgotten? I want a soul!"

The trees shake their branches; the wind tears off small twigs and throws them at us.

"Bring me a soul," she says, "and bring back the stone. It'll have done its purpose."

"What do you mean?"

She shakes her head. "You won't continue your walking. And you'll forget."

"And how do I come by a soul?" I lean toward her and try to smile. "Do I purchase one? Do I chase after one and try to catch it?"

"Questions! Questions!" She stomps her foot. "No more questions now!"

"All right." I sigh, take the stone from my bag, rub it, look at it, and put it back. "All right. Whatever happens, if it works, then it's a trade."

I stand in the moonlight by the mahogany desk and feel the stone against my throat.

In the living room the winds rush at me, dismember me. The walls become luminous, settle back into their true dimensions. I reach for the stone but see that the room lies dark and vacant and take my hand from my throat. The sofa, the television set, the chairs, and people are gone. All is empty; all is silent, and refuse litters the bare, wooden floor.

I dress in the morning, take the bus, and return to work.

"You're still looking pale," Virginia Hagerty says. "Are you sure you feel all right?"

"Look!" Claire Fields comes closer. "Look at the pretty necklace!"

I draw back when she raises her hand to touch the stone.

Darkness comes, yields to grey dawn, scatters dusk, and, again, the mist of morning rises. In the house I open all of the doors, walk among the litter and decay. In the library I slip into dark corners, try to hide in the back of the stacks. In passing, from the corners of my eyes, I see Virginia Hagerty and Claire Fields shake their heads.

Then, in the middle of the night, the house summons me, and I feel a strange excitement. The litter, the refuse are gone. The entrance hall is full of crates and boxes, and furniture stands in disarray. Newspaper is spread on the stairs; muddy tracks lead to the upper hall.

In my mother's bedroom two people lie close and breathe deeply. In my room a girl of about fifteen has thrown off the covers and shivers with cold. Another girl, younger, smaller, sleeps in the room where my father used to be. Her eyes move behind closed lids. One corner of her mouth is turned up and quivers slightly. I stand by her bed, turn to leave, then turn and look at her again.

In the nursery, in the corner by the window, a small boy of five or six lies with his cheek in the palm of his hand. I step out of the shadows into the light that falls over the head of his bed. His blond hair curls around his ear; his cheeks are flushed. I bend over him and touch his forehead. He moves, turns his face toward me, and opens his eyes. Again I touch him, put my hand on the top of his head. He looks at me and shrinks back into his pillows. The flush is gone from his face. I stroke his cheek lightly. The muscles work in his throat; his mouth is wide open, but only a tiny, broken whimper comes from him. His small hands clutch the covers to his chin and hold them tightly. I take his hands into mine. He opens his fists without resistance, lets go of the sheets. He looks at me, squeezes his eyes shut, and whimpers again.

I touch the stone and sit up in my bed. A small shadow cowers by my feet, and I know that, in the house, the boy is dreaming.

The streets are dark, deserted. I hurry toward the park. Behind me the shadow follows, and I stop and wait for him to catch up.

The old woman is already waiting. The shadow of the boy stands behind me, hides in the folds of my coat.

"A soul," I say. "Remember the bargain!"

She laughs. "As you've said, it's a trade."

The boy clings to my side. She bends down, beckons, coos, and, slowly, he drifts to her. I step back, turn, in a hurry to be gone.

But she calls after me. "The stone!" she shouts. "The stone!"

Quickly, I slip the chain from my neck, throw the stone toward her.

I fall into my bed, exhausted, shaking, feel cheated, know that the trade is not yet complete. But then sleep comes, embraces me gently, and takes me deep beyond all dreams.

When I enter the library Virginia Hagerty looks up from her desk. "Wow!" she says. "Wow! Look at you! What a change! I know you're feeling better. You've even got the color back in your cheeks."

Claire Fields walks over, looks at me, and smiles. "Hey!" she says. "You *are* looking better. Matter of fact, you're looking downright good. But where is your pretty necklace? You really should wear it today; it'd be a perfect match for the shade of your dress."

"Necklace?" I touch my throat, puzzled.

"You know, the one with the nice green stone."

"Oh," I say and try not to look confused. "That one."

"Well, anyway," Virginia says, "I'm glad you're all well again."

"So am I," says Claire. "You know, we really worried. Good Lord! What was the matter with you? Half the time you walked around like you were dreaming, and you hardly talked to us. You looked like you were sick, Julie, but we couldn't figure out what was wrong."

Was I sick? What was the matter? I frown. It's true: something seemed to have been wrong.

Steve Rasnic Tem is bearded, burly, and a frequent contributor to Shadows. *His forte as a writer is the ability to see the small things we take for granted and to make us look twice to be sure we know what we saw. That second look, however, is never pleasant, always unsettling.*

CRUTCHES

by Steve Rasnic Tem

A tap, a thump. A tap, a thump. Michael listened to his mother pacing her room with the crutch, just overhead. He had awakened to the sound, 3 A.M., and that was two hours ago. Two hours of steady pacing, and how many before that?

He slipped on his robe, trying not to awaken Doris, and climbed the stairs slowly. He paused on the landing, where a great bay window displayed the western slope of the Rockies, the dark houses at its base, and the slow drift of snow like sleep falling from the peak. A narrow road ran between Michael's borrowed house and those darkened houses, a passageway that held few cars this time of year. A few local vehicles, certainly, but as the snow season reached its height even they would no longer be venturing out. People in Elkins Park only took out their cars when they needed something from another town, or if they were going on vacation. Otherwise, most people walked. Or made their way cross-country on skis.

He reached the top of the stairs and looked at the bottom of her door. The light was still on, and now he could hear the tap-thump of her one crutch, although much fainter than it had been downstairs. Once again he blamed himself for dragging his mother up here, but they really had no other place to go. Joe Jensen had offered him the place rent-free for a year, just to take care of it, and Michael and Doris had both been out of work for almost two years at that point. *And afraid of failing again,* Michael thought, then shook himself irritably. Elkins Park did have its advantages—it was cheap to live here, and a quiet place for Doris to do her painting.

There was no energy left in the marriage; there hadn't been for some time. Lack of money only made it worse. At least sometimes money could buy the energy: concerts, plays, ski trips and the like. They seemed to have no more words for each other. And finally here, in this house, time had stopped completely. They didn't go forward, but with some relief Michael realized things weren't falling back, either.

He paused in front of the door, then knocked before gently swinging it open.

His mother stood by the window, gray hair hanging over her cheeks, her tattered housecoat bunched into odd, shapeless lumps; she appeared suspended from the one crutch like a broken scarecrow. A cigarette dangled from the front of her mouth, the long ash suspended impossibly from its tip.

"You'll burn yourself, Mother."

She reached up and jerked the cigarette out of her mouth. "I'm sorry," she said softly, and turned to the window.

Tap thump. A hollow sound, and for a moment Michael imagined that her entire leg was wood.

She had gone downhill fast since the accident. Their first day there—she had fallen through a rotten board in the front steps. Michael had thought, momentarily, of suing his good friend Joe, who had no homeowner's insurance for this old derelict, but his family wasn't the kind to sue. What happens, happens, as his mother had put it at the time.

She looked awful. The broken leg seemed to have sapped the strength from the rest of her body. He remembered the way it had swollen, so quickly, and even at the time it had seemed the swelling was draining her face, her eyes, her long narrow fingers, of their small store of vitality.

"You should try to get some rest," he said.

She looked at him as if he couldn't possibly know what he was talking about. Then she gazed out the window again. "I can't sleep."

"You look worried."

She gazed at him distractedly. "I'm going to be on this crutch for the rest of my life."

"That's nonsense. You're healing fine. You never let anything like this get you down before."

"I was never this old before. I can feel it, Michael. Something's different inside me. I won't be letting go of this crutch until the day I die."

Michael started to speak but thought better of it. At least she was up out of bed; she'd stayed in bed for a long time after the accident. She wouldn't even try. Then the town doctor brought the crutches—he said there was a man in town who carved them himself—and she'd pulled herself up on them, so at least she could pace. There was something about the crutches that moved her, pulled her right up out of bed. Michael'd seen the look on her face when the doctor brought them. As if they were arcane objects, mysterious and magical.

"You're scaring me, Mother." It was embarrassing to say, but he suddenly realized it was true.

"I don't mean to, son."

As he started down the stairs he noted the change in sound. She had taken the other crutch out of the closet and now she was using two.

Tap thump. Tap thump. Restless. Pacing.

Michael didn't get out of bed immediately the next morning. His wife was already up, and that made it easier for him to stay in bed. If she were still there in the room she would be able to see he wasn't really tired at all, and he'd feel too guilty to stay in bed. There was nothing to do. He should have been out looking for a job, he thought irritably, but he knew he wasn't going to even try for a while.

It was the same every day. The same thoughts, the same worries. The lack of energy. It was the sameness that was wearing him down. He thought it was the sameness that would finally kill him.

The same. Each day. Always. Tap. Tap. Thump.

Elkins Park was a poor place to find work in any case. The general store and gift shop, the trail guide center, were all run by people who had been in Elkins Park for some time. It seemed unlikely there would be any more openings. Most of them had no more on the ball than he did, but they'd gotten here first and settled. They wouldn't budge. Jacobs at the guide center was a failed lawyer. Matthews at the gift shop a failed crafts store owner. The gift shop was owned by a friend in Denver and he merely worked there.

Michael didn't know a single person in town who hadn't failed somewhere else. The realization troubled him. It was as if they had all gathered here. What was so attractive about this place?

The next day he had to go into town for supplies. Willis had had the grocery store in the Park for over ten years. But before that he had had a chain, ten of them all along the front range. He'd lost them all in little over two years. Tap. When Michael walked through the door . . . tap . . . Willis looked up and smiled wanly. Thump. He had a crutch. Michael wasn't surprised.

"What can I get for you today, Michael?" Tap tap.

Not wanting to talk to the man, Michael just handed him Doris's list. Thump.

While Willis was filling the order Michael wandered out onto the wide wooden boardwalk fronting the store. The day already seemed to have turned cooler since the morning. He hunched his shoulders inside his jacket and turned to walk down the street. But the sight of dozens of crutches stacked haphazardly in the alley next to the store stopped him.

A bearded man in a checkered shirt lumbered into view, rearranging the crutches into a neat stack. Michael could see now that the crutches looked handcarved—like the others he had seen around town, like the kind his mother had—each one slightly different.

The big man stopped and stared at Michael, seeming to appraise him, then returned to his workbench set up deeper in the alley.

"Hey, wait!" Michael cried, and ran after him.

The man picked up a rough-shaped crutch and began smoothing it with knife and sandpaper.

"What are you doing?"

The man edged a crutch forward to the front of the bench. "Crutches," he said.

Michael peered at the man. He could swear there were tears in his eyes. "Everybody needs a crutch now and then, eh?" He wasn't sure why he said it. "Can I buy a pair?" he asked, and immediately regretted it.

"I only sell one at a time," the man said quietly. "And you don't seem to need one, not just yet."

Michael glanced away. The man was grinning now. "You think this a pretty good joke, don't you!" Michael suddenly shouted, and slammed his fist on the crutch on the bench. It snapped like a twig. Michael's eyes widened. "Why . . . why it wouldn't support a kitten!" he cried.

Tap. The man said nothing. Tap. After an awkward moment, Michael turned and left.

He drove home quickly, trying not to glance at pedestrians. But every now and then he couldn't help looking to the side and seeing that a quarter of the people were using crutches. Tap tap. Tap tap.

Workers were renovating an old house on the outskirts, just before the turnoff to Michael's own residence. Hammer shots echoed in the winter stillness. Tap tap tap tap. He tried to ignore the sound. Beams had been propped up against one side; the house leaned precariously, as if the beams were all that held it erect.

One of the workers pulled tools out of a metal box, then tossed them one at a time into the tall weeds behind the structure. Then he sat down on the box and rubbed his legs.

Michael drove more slowly the rest of the way home, afraid he might miss something. Something was happening in Elkins Park.

When he got home he found all of Doris's painting supplies in the trash, along with most of her paintings. He picked them out one at a time, sadly, examining torn canvas and broken frames. Some of her best work: that old lady back in the city, her grandfather's house, Michael's own portrait.

She was sitting on the couch in the living room, watching television. "Why'd you do it, Doris?" he asked, feeling uneasy about the trembling in his voice.

"I'm giving it up, Michael. There just isn't any point." She looked years older than she had that morning. Tap. Michael was numbed. How could someone change so drastically in the course of one day?

"You've felt discouraged before . . ." Tap.

"It's different this time. I have nothing to paint about, nothing to say." Tap. "Painting is about the last thing I want to be doing with my time." She turned her head and locked her eyes onto the television screen.

Michael watched her face glaze over. "So what do you want to do with your time?" He knew it must sound sarcastic. Tap. But she didn't react. Tap. It was as if she hadn't even heard him.

Suddenly she was looking up at the ceiling. Examining it. As if she were looking for the point of contact of his mother's crutch and the floor. Tap. As if she might *see* the sound. Her eyes out of focus, glazed.

His mother hung over the bed, her hips and belly gone to fat. She glided over the covers, and suddenly it seemed to Michael that she was a great dark poisonous spider. He stared at the wall and moaned. It was true . . . the shadow had eight legs. He turned to see her creeping up over his face, and was almost relieved to see it wasn't his mother at all but a small spider made larger in shadow by the porch light, crawling up his bedclothes. But then he looked more closely and saw that the spider had no legs at all but eight crutches supporting its fat, limp abdomen . . .

In the morning, when he opened the front door to receive the mail from the carrier, he saw that the bearded young man was leaning weakly on a crutch. "Won't be coming out here anymore; they'll have to replace me. See, my leg here . . ."

Michael shut the door in his face.

He normally worked around the house on Saturdays, then read out on the enclosed front porch. But he couldn't bear to be there that weekend; he couldn't sit still: Doris with the TV going the whole time, staring at it silently, his mother pacing with her two crutches in hollow syncopation on the loose floorboards. He saw the way Doris watched his mother sometimes now—the glow of excitement in her eyes. Following the movement of crutch, arm, and leg as if it were some sort of ballet. Tap thump. Tap thump. The noise wasn't very loud, but he found it impossible to ignore. He found himself listening for it, focusing his hearing, holding his breath until he could make out the faint tap tap thump, becoming more and more irritated.

Michael threw down the paperback and got into his coat. He opened the door, hesitated at the first blast of sharp cold wind, then plunged ahead. And almost jumped at the sound of the screen door bouncing off the inner door. Tap tap tap tap. Following him.

He had no idea where he was going. The snow made the road all but impassable; there would be virtually no traffic. About a half mile before town he looked off toward the Carter place up on the hill. A tiny figure in a red coat, shoveling snow. It looked awkward, crippled. Michael shielded his eyes, squinted, and could just make out the crutch wedged under one arm.

He turned and picked up his pace toward town. And saw someone not more than ten yards ahead of him, standing by the side of the road.

A large bearded man. With an armful of crutches. Michael turned . . .

Tap tap tap tap behind him.

Michael was out of breath by the time he got back to the house, his lungs almost splitting from the cold and exhaustion. He couldn't quite see the details of the room once he stepped through the door; the snow had blinded him. But he heard it. Tap thump. Tap thump. With a slight variation in rhythm. Two slightly different rhythms.

He walked into the kitchen.

"Hello, son." His mother's tired voice. Tap.

"Michael?" Tap tap tap.

As his vision cleared he could see them by the stove—wife and mother. Doris had borrowed his mother's second crutch. They stared at him. And he couldn't bring himself to speak.

She woke him up in the middle of the night, every night the next few nights. Tap. Hobbling into the bathroom. Tap tap. Going to the kitchen for some milk. Thump. Letting the cat in. Tap thump. Doris, or his mother—he soon lost track. His mother pacing. Doris moving. Back and forth in the darkened house. The syncopation of their crutches. The synchrony.

Tap thump. Tap thump. No peace. No peace.

After the snow melted that year he was able to walk in the woods again. Until the little boys and girls drove him out. The children were the worst. On their crutches. Breaking their dogs' legs so they could strap on miniature crutches. Tap and tap and tap in every alley, on every sidewalk. The bearded man made them, as he made all the crutches; Michael had seen him pass them out to the kids. The kids just playing with their pets. But when they ran out of dogs, they started putting even smaller crutches on the cats. Then they were out in the woods, looking for squirrels, birds, anything they could catch; bundles of tiny crutches bunched in their fists like flowers.

Michael stopped pretending to seek work and spent most of his time hiding from his neighbors. He hadn't been bothered yet, but he was the only one in town without a crutch. It made him uneasy, and now he was seeing the large bearded man and his evil-looking sticks of wood everywhere he went.

Doris certainly didn't notice; she didn't notice him at all these days. Unless he stood in front of the TV.

Each night he awakened from a fever dream. Suddenly he was frightened. He could not remember how long he had lived in the town, if he had lived in the town forever, if he would be returning to the city after the summer. If he had ever lived in the city at all. His wife slept untroubled beside him, her shoulders, her shadowed face seeming older than he remembered. Had she aged so much? Had they been there that long?

He stands up out of sleep and reaches for the bedpost. It is soft wood. Seductive. He pats it. Tap tap tap it replies. Thump. There is energy in the wood. The first energy, the first aliveness, he has encountered in some time. And he is so tired, and his life is so much the same, again and again the same. He has no energy.

He runs his hands down the sides of the wood and is soothed by it. He turns to the bedroom window and sees the face of the bearded man behind the glass. Grinning. Tap tap tapping with two stubby fingers against the glass. And amazingly, Michael realizes he is not afraid. He strokes the wood, taps it. It is vaguely comforting and he thinks, tap tap, maybe, tap tap tap, tomorrow it might support him.

*Pat Cadigan writes verse for Hallmark for a living. In what little
spare time she has, however, she co-edits the impressive fantasy
magazine* Shayol *with her husband, Arnie Fenner, and has become one of the brightest new talents in the sf and fantasy fields.
Those of you living in New England may recognize the setting;
the game, on the other hand . . .*

EENIE, MEENIE, IPSATEENIE

by Pat Cadigan

In the long, late summer afternoons in the alley behind the
tenement where Milo Sinclair had lived, the pavement smelled
baked and children's voices carried all over the neighborhood.
The sky, cracked by TV aerials, was *blue*, the way it never is after
you're nine years old and in the parking lot of La Conco D'Oro
Restaurant the garlic-rich aroma of Siciliano cooking was always
heavy in the air.

It had never been that way for the boy walking down the alley
beside Milo. La Conco D'Oro didn't exist anymore; the cool,
coral-tinted interior Milo had glimpsed when he'd been a kid
now held a country-western bar, ludicrous in a small industrial
New England town. He smiled down at the boy a little sadly. The
boy grinned back. He was much smaller than Milo remembered
being at the same age. He also remembered the world being
bigger. The fence around Mr. Parillo's garden had been several
inches higher than his head. He paused at the spot where the
garden had been, picturing it in front of the brown and tan
Parillo house where the irascible old gardener had been landlord
to eleven other families. The Parillo house was worse than just
gone—the city was erecting a smacking new apartment house on
the spot. The new building was huge, its half-finished shell
spreading over to the old parking lot where the bigger boys had
sometimes played football. He looked at the new building with
distaste. It had a nice clean brick facade and would probably hold
a hundred families in plasterboard box rooms. Several yards back
up the alley, his old tenement stood, empty now, awaiting the

wrecking ball. No doubt another erstwhile hundred-family dwelling would rise there, too.

Beside Milo, the boy was fidgeting in an innocent, patient way. Some things never changed. Kids never held still, never had, never would. They'd always fumble in their pants pockets and shift their weight from one foot to the other, just the way the boy was doing. Milo gazed thoughtfully at the top of the white-blond head. His own sandy hair had darkened a good deal, though new grey was starting to lighten it again.

Carelessly, the boy kicked at a pebble. His sneaker laces flailed the air. "Hey," said Milo. "Your shoelaces came untied."

The boy was unconcerned. "Yeah, they always do."

"You could trip on 'em, knock your front teeth out. That wouldn't thrill your mom too much. Here." Milo crouched on one knee in front of the boy. "I'll tie 'em for you so they'll stay tied."

The boy put one sneaker forward obligingly, almost touching Milo's shoe. It was a white sneaker with a thick rubber toe. And Milo remembered again how it had been that last long late summer afternoon before he and his mother had moved away.

There in the alley behind Water Street, in Water St. Lane, when the sun hung low and the shadows stretched long, they had all put their feet in, making a dirty canvas rosette, Milo and Sammy and Stevie, Angie, Kathy, Flora and Bonnie, for Rhonda to count out. Rhonda always did the counting because she was the oldest. She tapped each foot with a strong index finger, chanting the formula that would determine who would be IT for a game of hide-'n-seek.

> *Eenie, meenie, ipsateenie*
> *Goo, gah, gahgoleenie*
> *Ahchee, pahchee, Liberaci*
> *Out goes Y-O-U!*

Stevie pulled his foot back. He was thin like Milo but taller and freckled all over. Protestant. His mother was living with someone who wasn't his father. The Sicilian tongues wagged and wagged. Stevie didn't care. At least he didn't have an oddball name like Milo and he never had to get up for church on Sunday. His black

high-top sneakers were P.F. Flyers for running faster and jumping higher.

Eenie, meenie, ipsateenie . . .

Nobody said anything while Rhonda chanted. When she
counted you, you stayed counted and you kept quiet. Had
Rhonda been the first to say *Let's play hide-'n-seek?* Milo didn't
know. Suddenly all of them had been clamoring to play, all except him. He hated hide-'n-seek, especially just before dark,
which was when they all wanted to play most. It was the only
time for hide-'n-seek, Rhonda always said. It was more fun if it
was getting dark. He hated it, but if you didn't play you might as
well go home, and it was too early for that. Besides, the moving
van was coming tomorrow. Aunt Syl would be driving him and
his mother to the airport. He might not play anything again for
months. But why did they have to play hide-'n-seek?

Out goes Y-O-U!

Kathy slid her foot out of the circle. She was never IT. She was
Rhonda's sister, almost too young to play. She always cried if she
lost a game. Everyone let her tag the goal so she wouldn't cry and
go home to complain Rhonda's friends were picking on her,
bringing the wrath of her mother down on them. Her mother
would bust up the game. Milo wished she'd do that now, appear
on the street drunk in her housedress and slippers, the way she
did sometimes, and scream Rhonda and Kathy home. Then
they'd have to play something else. He didn't like any of them
when they were playing hide-'n-seek. Something happened to
them when they were hiding, something not very nice. Just by
hiding, they became *different*, in a way Milo could never understand or duplicate. All of them hid better than he could, so he
always ended up being found last, which meant that he had to be
IT. He had to go look for them, then; he was the hunter. But not
really. Searching for them in all the dark places, the deep places
where they crouched breathing like animals, waiting to jump out
at him, he knew they were all the hunters and he was the prey. It
was just another way for them to hunt him. And when he found
them, when they exploded from their hiding places lunging at
him, all pretense of his being the hunter dropped away and he

ran, ran like hell and hoped it was fast enough, back to the goal to tag it ahead of them. Otherwise he'd have to be IT all over again and the things he found squatting under stairs and behind fences became a little worse than before, a little more powerful.

Out goes Y-O-U!

Sammy's sneaker scraped the pavement as he dragged it out of the circle. Sammy was plump around the edges, the baby fat he had carried all his life melting away. He wore Keds, at war with Stevie's P.F. Flyers to see who could *really* run faster and jump higher. Sammy could break your arm. Milo didn't want to have to look for him. He'd never be able to outrun Sammy. He stared at Rhonda's fuzzy brown head bent over their feet with the intentness of a jeweler counting diamonds. He tried to will her to count him out next. If he could just make it through one game without having to be IT, then it might be too late to play another. They would all have to go home when the streetlights came on. Tomorrow he would leave and never have to find any of them again.

Out goes Y-O-U!

Bonnie. Then Flora. They came and went together in white sneakers and blue Bermuda shorts, Bonnie the follower and Flora the leader. You could tell that right away by Flora's blue cat's-eye glasses. Bonnie was chubby, ate a lot of pasta, smelled like sauce. Flora was wiry from fighting with her five brothers. She was the one who was always saying you could hear Milo coming a mile away because of his housekeys. They were pinned inside his pocket on a Good Luck key chain from Pleasure Island, and they jingled when he ran. He put his hand down deep in his pocket and clutched the keys in his sweaty fist.

Out goes Y-O-Me!

Rhonda was safe. Now it was just Milo and Angie, like a duel between them with Rhonda's finger pulling the trigger. Angie's dark eyes stared out of her pointy little face. She was a thin girl, all sharp angles and sharp teeth. Her dark brown hair was caught up in a confident ponytail. If he were IT, she would be waiting for him more than any of the others, small but never frightened.

Milo gripped his keys tighter. None of them were ever frightened. It wasn't fair.

Out goes Y-O-U!

Milo backed away, his breath exploding out of him in relief. Angie pushed her face against the wall of the tenement, closing her eyes and throwing her arms around her head to show she wasn't peeking. She began counting toward one hundred by fives, loud, so everyone could hear. You couldn't stop it now. Milo turned and fled, pounding down the alley until he caught up with Stevie and Sammy.

"Don't follow us!" "Your keys are jingling!" "Milo, you always get caught, bug off!" Stevie and Sammy ran faster, but he kept up with them all the way across the parking lot down to Middle Street, where they ducked into a narrow space between two buildings. Milo slipped past them so Stevie was closest to the outside. They stood with their backs to the wall like little urban guerrillas, listening to the tanky echoes of their panting.

"She coming?" Milo whispered after a minute.

"How the hell should we know, think we got X-ray vision?" "Why'd you have to come with us, go hide by yourself, sissy-piss!"

Milo didn't move. If he stayed with them, maybe they wouldn't change into the nasty things. Maybe they'd just want to hurry back and tag the goal fast so they could get rid of him.

Far away Angie shouted, "Ready or not, here I come, last one found is IT!" Milo pressed himself hard against the wall, wishing he could melt into it like Casper the Friendly Ghost. They'd never find him if he could walk through walls. But he'd always be able to see them, no matter where they hid. They wouldn't make fun of him then. He wouldn't need his housekeys anymore, either, so they'd never know when he was coming up behind them. They'd be scared instead of him.

"My goal one-two-three!" Kathy's voice was loud and mocking. She'd just stuck near the goal again so she could tag it the minute Angie turned her back. Angie wouldn't care. She was looking for everyone else and saving Milo for last.

"She coming?" Milo asked again.

Sammy's eyes flickered under half-closed lids. Suddenly his hand clamped onto Milo's arm, yanking him around to Stevie, who shoved him out onto the sidewalk. Milo stumbled, doing a horrified little dance as he tried to scramble back into hiding. Sammy and Stevie blocked his way.

"Guess she isn't. Coming." Sammy smiled. Milo retreated, bumping into a car parked at the curb as they came out and walked past him. He followed, keeping a careful distance. They went up the street past the back of Mr. Parillo's to the yard behind the rented cottage with the grapevine. Sammy and Stevie stopped at the driveway. Milo waited behind them.

The sunlight was redder, hot over the cool wind springing up from the east. The day was dying. Sammy nodded. He and Stevie headed silently up the driveway to a set of cool stone steps by the side door of the cottage. The steps led to a skinny passage between the cottage and Bonnie's father's garage that opened at the alley directly across from the goal. They squatted at the foot of the steps, listening. Up ahead, two pairs of sneakers pattered on asphalt.

"My goal one-two-three!" "My goal one-two-three!" Flora and Bonnie together. Where was Angie? Sammy crawled halfway up the steps and peeked over the top.

"See her?" Milo asked.

Sammy reached down and hauled him up by his shirt collar, holding him so the top step jammed into his stomach.

"*You* see her, Milo? Huh? She there?" Sammy snickered as Milo struggled out of his grasp and slid down the steps, landing on Stevie, who pushed him away.

"Rhonda's goal one-two-three!" Angie's voice made Sammy duck down quickly.

"Shit!" Rhonda yelled.

"Don't swear! I'm tellin'!"

"Oh, shut up, you say it, too, who're you gonna tell anyway?"

"Your mother!"

"She says it, too, tattletale!"

"Swearer!"

Milo crept closer to Stevie again. If he could just avoid Angie till the streetlights came on, everything would be all right. "She still there?" he asked.

Stevie crawled up the steps and had a look. After a few seconds he beckoned to Sammy. "Let's go."

Sammy gave Stevie a few moments headstart and then followed.

Milo stood up. "Sammy?"

Sammy paused to turn, plant one of his Keds on Milo's chest, and shove. Milo jumped backward, lost his balance, and sat down hard in the dirt. Sammy grinned at him as though this were part of a prank they were playing on everyone else. When he was sure Milo wouldn't try to get up, he turned and went down the passage. Milo heard him and Stevie tag their goals together. He closed his eyes.

The air was becoming deeper, cooler, clearer. Sounds carried better now. Someone wished on the first star.

"That's an airplane, stupid!"

"Is not, it's the first star!"

And then Angie's voice, not sounding the least bit out of breath, as though she'd been waiting quietly for Milo to appear after Sammy. "Where's Milo?"

He sprang up and ran. Sammy would tell where they'd been hiding and she'd come right for him. He sprinted across Middle Street, cut between the nurse's house and the two-family place where the crazy man beat his wife every Thursday to Middle St. Lane. Then down to Fourth Street and up to the corner where it met Middle a block away from the Fifth Street bridge.

They were calling him. He could hear them shouting his name, trying to fool him into thinking the game was over, and he kept out of sight behind the house on the corner. Two boys went by on bikes, coasting leisurely. Milo waited until they were well up the street before dashing across to the unpaved parking area in front of the apartment house where the fattest woman in town sat on her porch and drank a quart of Coke straight from the bottle every afternoon. There was a garbage shed next to the house. The Board of Health had found rats there once, come up from the polluted river running under the bridge. Milo crouched behind the shed and looked cautiously up the alley.

They were running back and forth, looking, listening for the jingle of his keys. "He *was* back there with us!" "Spread out, we'll find him!" "Maybe he sneaked home." "Nah, he couldn't." "Everybody look for him!" They all scattered except for Kathy, bored and playing a lazy game of hopscotch under a streetlight that hadn't come on yet.

Impulsively Milo snatched open the door of the shed and squeezed in between two overflowing trash barrels. The door flapped shut by itself, closing him in with a ripe garbagey smell and the keening of flies. He stood very still, eyes clenched tightly, and his arms crossed over his chest. They'd never think he was in here. Not after the rats.

Thick footsteps approached and stopped. Milo felt the presence almost directly in front of the shed. Lighter steps came from another direction and there was the scrape of sand against rubber as someone turned around and around, searching.

"He's gotta be somewhere." Sammy. "I didn't think the little bastard could run *that* fast." Milo could sense the movement of Sammy's head disturb the air. The flies sang louder. "We'll get him. He's gonna be IT."

"Call 'olly, olly, out-free.'" Stevie.

"Nah. Then he won't have to be IT."

"Call it and then say we had our fingers crossed so it doesn't count."

"Let's look some more. If we still can't find him, then we'll call it."

"He's a sissy-piss."

They went away. When the footsteps faded, Milo came out cautiously, choking from the smell in the shed. He stood listening to the sound of the neighborhood growing quieter. Darkness flowed up from the east more quickly now, reaching for the zenith, eager to spill itself down into the west and blot out the last bit of sunlight. Above the houses a star sparkled and winked, brightening. Milo gazed up at it, wishing as hard as he could.

> *Star light, star bright*
> *First star I see tonight*
> *I wish I may, I wish I might*
> *Have this wish . . .*
> *Eenie, meenie, ipsateenie . . .*
> *Don't let me be IT.*

He stood straining up at the star. Just this once. If he wouldn't have to be IT. If he could be safe. Just this once—

"Angie! Angie! Down here, quick!"

He whirled and found Flora pointing at him, jumping up and down as she shouted. *No!* he wanted to scream. But Flora kept yelling for Angie to hurry, *hurry,* she could still get him before the streetlights came on. He fled to Middle Street, across Fourth to the next block, going toward the playground. There was nowhere to hide there among the swings and seesaws, but there was an empty house next to it. Without much hope, Milo ran up the back steps and pushed at the door.

He found himself sprawling belly-down on the cracking kitchen linoleum. Blinking, he got to his feet. There was no furniture, no curtains in the windows. He tried to remember who had lived there last, the woman with the funny-looking dogs or the two queer guys? He went to one of the windows and then ducked back. Angie was coming down the sidewalk alone, smiling to herself. She passed the house, her ponytail bobbing along behind her. Milo tiptoed into the living room, keeping close to the wall. Shadows spread from the corners, unpenetrated by the last of the daylight coming through the windows and the three tiny panes over the front door. He ran to the door and pulled at it desperately, yanking himself back and forth like a yo-yo going sideways.

"Milo?"

He clung to the door, holding his breath. He had left the back door open and she was in the kitchen. The floor groaned as she took one step and then another. "I know you're hiding in here, Milo." She laughed.

Behind him were stairs leading to the second floor. He moved to them silently and began to crawl upward, feeling years of grit in the carpet runner scraping his hands and knees.

"You're gonna be IT now, Milo." He heard her walk as far as the entrance to the living room and then stop.

Milo kept crawling. If the streetlights went on now, it wouldn't make any difference. You couldn't see them in here. But maybe she'd give up and go away, if he could stay in the dark where she couldn't see him. She had to see him, actually lay eyes on him, before she could run back and tag his goal.

"Come on, Milo. Come on out. I know you're here. We're not

supposed to be in here. If you come out now, I'll race you to the goal. You might even win."

He knew he wouldn't. She'd have Sammy waiting for him, ready to tackle him and hold him down so Angie could get to the goal first. Sammy would tackle him and Stevie would sit on him while everyone else stood and laughed and laughed and laughed. Because then he'd have to be IT forever. No matter where he went, they'd always be hiding, waiting to jump out at him, forcing him to find them again and again and again and he'd never get away from them. Every time he turned a corner, one of them would be there yelling. *You're IT, you're IT!*

"What are you afraid of, Milo? Are you afraid of a girl? Milo's a fraidycat! 'Fraid of a girl, 'fraid of a girl!" She giggled. He realized she was in the middle of the living room now. All she had to do was look up to see him between the bars of the staircase railing. He put his hand on the top step and pulled himself up very slowly, praying the stairs wouldn't creak. His pants rubbed the dirty runner with a sandpapery sound.

"Wait till I tell everyone you're scared of a *girl*. And you'll still be IT, and everyone will know." Milo drew back into the deep shadows on the second-floor landing. He heard her move to the bottom of the stairs and put her foot on the first step. "No matter where you go, everyone will know," she singsonged. "No matter where you go, everyone will know. Milo's IT, Milo's IT."

He wrapped his arms around his knees, pulling himself into a tight ball. In his pocket the housekeys dug into the fold between his hip and thigh.

"You'll have to take your turn sometime, Milo. Even if you move away everyone will know you're IT. They'll all hide from you. No one will play with you. You'll always be IT. Always and always."

He dug in his heels and pushed himself around to the doorway of one of the bedrooms. Maybe she wouldn't be able to see him in the darkness and she'd go away. Then he could go home.

"I heard you. I heard you move. Now I know where you are. I'm gonna find you, Milo." She came up the last steps, groping in the murky shadows. He could just make out the shape of her head and her ponytail.

"Got you!" She sprang at him like a trap. "You're IT!"

"No!"

Milo kicked out. The darkness spun around him. For several seconds he felt her grabbing his arms and legs, trying to pull him out of hiding before her clutching hands fell away and her laughter was replaced by a series of thudding, crashing noises.

On hands and knees, panting like a dog, he crept to the edge of the top step and looked down. Angie's small form was just visible where it lay at the foot of the stairs. Her legs were still on the steps. The rest of her was spread on the floor with her head tilted at a questioning angle. Milo waited for her to get up crying, *You pushed me, I'm telling!* but she never moved. Slowly he went halfway down the stairs, clinging to the rickety bannister.

"Angie?"

She didn't answer. He descended the rest of the way, careful to avoid her legs in case she suddenly came to life and tried to kick him.

"Angie?"

He knelt beside her. Her eyes were open, staring through him at nothing. He waited for her to blink or twitch, but she remained perfectly still. Milo didn't touch her. *She'd have done it to me,* he thought. She would have, too. She'd have pushed him down the stairs to get to the goal first. After all, Sammy had kicked him off the other stairs so he couldn't touch goal with him and Stevie. Now they were even. Sort of. Sammy had been on her side, after all. Milo stood up. She wouldn't chase him anymore and she'd never touch his goal on him.

He found his way to the back door, remembering to close it as he left. For a few moments he stood in the yard, trying to find the star he had wished on. Others were beginning to come out now. But the streetlights—something must be wrong with them, he thought. The city had forgotten about them. Or maybe there was a power failure. He should have wished for them to come on. That would have sent everyone home.

While he stood there, the streetlights did come on, like eyes opening everywhere all over the neighborhood. Milo's shoulders slumped with relief. Now he really had won. Everyone had to go home now. The game was over. It was over and he wouldn't have to be IT.

He ran through the playground, across Water St. Lane and up Water, getting home just as the final pink glow in the west died.

"There." Milo finished tying a double bow in the boy's shoelaces. "Now they won't come undone."

The boy frowned at his feet critically. "How'm I gonna get 'em off?"

"Like this." Milo demonstrated for him. "See?" He retied the bow. "It's easy when you get the hang of it."

"Maybe I'll just leave 'em on when I go to bed."

"And when you take a bath, too?" Milo laughed. "Sneakers in the tub'll go over real well with your mom."

"I won't take baths. Just wipe off with a washcloth."

Milo restrained himself from looking behind the kid's ears. Instead, he stood up and began walking again. The boy stayed beside him, trying to whistle between his teeth and only making a rhythmic hissing noise. Milo could have sympathized. He'd never learned to whistle very well himself. Even today his whistle had more air than tune in it. Sammy had been a pretty good whistler. He'd even been able to whistle between his fingers like the bigger boys. Stevie hadn't been able to, but Sammy hadn't made fun of him the way he'd made fun of Milo.

Milo half-expected to see Sammy and Stevie as he and the boy approached the spot where the garbage shed had been. Now there was a modern dumpster there, but Milo imagined that the rats could get into that easily enough if any cared to leave the river. Aunt Syl had written his mother that environmentalists had forced the city to clean up the pollution, making it more livable for the rats under the bridge.

But the dumpster was big enough for someone Sammy's size to hide behind. Or in. Milo shook his head. Sammy's size? Sammy was all grown up now, just like he was. All of them were all grown up now. Except Angie. Angie was still the same age she'd been on that last day, he knew that for a fact. Because she'd never stopped chasing him.

It took her a long, long time to find him because he had broken the rule about leaving the neighborhood. You weren't supposed to leave the neighborhood to hide. You weren't supposed to go home, either, and he had done that, too.

But then he'd thought the game was really over. He'd thought it had ended at the bottom of the stairs in the vacant house with the daylight's going and the streetlights' coming on. Rhonda had been the last one found, the *only* one found, so she should have been IT, not Milo. The next game should have gone on without him. Without him and Angie, of course. He thought it had. All through the long, dull ride to the airport and the longer, duller flight from New England to the Midwest, through the settling in at the first of the new apartments and the settling down to passable if lackluster years in the new school, he thought the game had continued without him and Angie.

But the night came when he found himself back in that darkening empty house, halfway up the stairs to the second floor. He froze in the act of reaching for the next step, feeling the dirt and fear and approach of IT.

When the floor creaked, he screamed and woke himself up before he could hear the sound of her childish, taunting voice. He was flat on his back in bed, gripping the covers in a stranglehold. After a few moments he sat up and wiped his hands over his face.

The room was quiet and dark, much darker than the house had been that last day. He got up without turning on the light and went to the only window. This was the fourth apartment they'd had since coming to the Midwest, but they'd all been the same. Small, much smaller than the one in the tenement, done in plaster ticky-tacky with too few windows. Modern housing in old buildings remodeled for modern living with the woodwork painted white. At least the apartment was on the eighth floor. Milo preferred living high up. You could see everything from high up. Almost.

The street that ran past the building gleamed wetly under the streetlights. It had rained. He boosted the window up and knelt before the sill, listening to the moist sighing of occasional passing cars. A damp breeze puffed through the screen.

Across the street something moved just out of the bright circle the streetlight threw on the sidewalk.

When the streetlights came on, it was time to go home.

A stray dog. It was probably just a stray dog over there. In the distance, a police siren wailed and then cut off sharply. Milo's mouth was dry as he squinted through the screen. It was too late for kids to be out.

But if you didn't get home after the streetlights came on, did that mean you never had to go home ever?

The movement came again, but he still couldn't see it clearly. A shadow was skirting the patch of light on the pavement, dipping and weaving, but awkwardly, stiffly. It wanted to play, but there was no one awake to play with, except for Milo.

He spread his fingers on the windowsill and lowered his head. It was too late for kids to be out. Any kids. The streetlights—

Something flashed briefly in the light and then retreated into the darkness. Milo's sweaty fingers slipped on the sill. The game was over. He wasn't IT. He wasn't. She'd found him but she hadn't tagged his goal and all the streetlights had come on. The game was over, had been over for years. It wasn't fair.

The figure made another jerky movement. He didn't have to see it clearly now to know about the funny position of its head, its neck still crooked in that questioning angle, the lopsided but still confident bobbing of the ponytail, the dirty-white sneakers. Another police siren was howling through the streets a few blocks away, but it didn't quite cover up the sound of a little girl's voice, singing softly because it was so late.

> *Eenie, meenie, ipsateenie*
> *Goo, gah, gahgoleenie*
> *Ahchee, pahchee, Liberaci*
> *Out goes Y-O-U!*
> *Eenie, meenie, ipsateenie*
> *Goo, gah, gahgoleenie . . .*

He covered his ears against it, but he could still hear it mocking him. No one was being counted out, no one would ever be counted out again because he was IT and he had missed his turn.

Come out, Milo. Come out, come out, come out. You're IT.

He pressed his hands tighter against his ears, but it only shut the sound of her voice up in his head and made it louder. Then he was clawing at the screen, yelling, "I'm not! I'm not! I'm not IT, the game's over and *I'm not IT!*"

His words hung in the air, spiraling down around him. There

was a soft pounding on the wall behind the bed. "Milo!" came his mother's muffled, sleepy voice. "It's four in the morning, what are you screaming for?"

He sank down onto the floor, leaning his head hopelessly against the windowsill. "A, a dream, Mom," he said, his voice hoarse and thick in his tight throat. "Just a bad dream."

The wind poured through his hair, chilling the sweat that dripped down to his neck. Laughter came in with the wind, light, careless, jeering laughter. He knew Angie was looking up at his window, her sharp little teeth bared in a grin.

" 'Fraid of a girl," the laughter said. " 'Fraid of a girl . . ."

The boy was staring at his pants pocket and Milo realized he'd been jingling his loose change without thinking as they walked. He thought about giving the kid a quarter, but his mother had probably warned him not to take candy or money from strangers. Most likely he wasn't even supposed to talk to strangers. But most kids were too curious not to. They were programmed to answer questions from adults anyway, so all you had to do was ask them something and pretty soon you were carrying on a regular conversation. As long as you didn't make the mistake of offering them any money or candy, the kids figured they were safe.

"Housekeys," Milo lied, jingling the change some more. "When I was your age, my mother pinned them inside my pocket and they jingled whenever I ran."

"How come she did that?"

"She worked. My father was dead. I had to let myself in and out when she wasn't home and she didn't want me to lose my keys."

The boy accepted that without comment. Absent fathers were more common now anyway. The boy probably knew a lot of kids who carried housekeys, if he wasn't carrying any himself.

"She pin 'em in there today?"

"What?" Milo blinked at him.

"Your housekeys." The boy grinned insolently.

Milo gave him half a smile. Some things never changed. Kids still thought a joke at someone else's expense was funny. He glanced down at the double bows he'd tied in the boy's laces. Yeah, he could picture one of those sneakers on some other kid's chest, kicking him off some steps. The boy looked more like

Stevie than Sammy, but that didn't matter. Stevie would have done it if he'd had the chance. Milo was sure this boy would have been great friends with Angie.

They were past the dumpster, almost to the corner where Water St. Lane crossed Fourth. The house where the fattest woman in town had consumed her daily quart of Coke straight from the bottle was still inhabited. Somewhere inside, a radio was boasting that it had the hits, all the hits and nothing but the hits. Milo didn't think it would be long before this house stood as empty as his old tenement, condemned and waiting to fall. It wasn't about to collapse by itself. These old houses had been built to stay up, no matter how tired and shabby they became. Endurance, that was what it was. But anything could reach the end of its endurance eventually—a neighborhood, a building, a person. Neighborhoods and buildings had to be taken care of, but people could take things into their own hands. You didn't have to endure something past the point when it should have ended. Not if you knew what to do.

Milo hadn't known what to do at first though. He found himself helpless again, as helpless as he'd been on those old stairs so many years ago. In the dream or wide-awake, crouched at his bedroom window while the little-girl thing that hadn't made it home before dark played on the sidewalk and called him, he was helpless. Angie didn't care that Rhonda should have been IT. Rhonda and the others had gone home after the streetlights had come on, but he and Angie hadn't. The game wasn't done even though it was just the two of them now.

Slowly he began to realize it was the other kids. One of the bigger boys with the bikes must have seen him climb into the car with his mother and Aunt Syl the next day and passed it on to another kid who passed it on to another kid in a long, long game of *Gossip* that stretched over hundreds and hundreds of miles, with Angie following, free to leave the neighborhood because he had, free to stay out late because she had never gone home. Angie, following him all the way to the Midwest, to the new neighborhood, to the new apartment because of the new kids at the new school who had been happy to tell her where he was because everyone loved a good hunt. The new kids, they were all just Sammys and Stevies and Floras and Bonnies with different names and faces anyway. They all knew he was IT and had missed his turn. Even his mother knew something; she looked at him strangely sometimes when she thought he didn't know, and he could feel her waiting for him to tell her, explain. But he couldn't possibly. She had taken her turn a long time ago, just like all the adults, and when you took your turn, you forgot. She couldn't have understood if he had explained until the day he died.

So he'd held out for a long, long time and they moved to new apartments, but Angie always found him. Kids were everywhere and they always told on him. And then one day he looked at himself and found Milo staring out at him from a grown-up face, a new hiding place for the little boy with the same old fear. And he thought, *Okay; okay. We'll end it now, for you and for Angie.* He was big now, and he hadn't forgotten. He would help little Milo still helpless inside of him, still hiding from Angie.

He went back. Back to the old neighborhood, taking Angie up on her offer of a race to the goal at last.

Deep summer. The feel of it had hit him the moment he'd walked down to the alley from the bus stop at Third and Water, where most of the old buildings were still standing all the way down to St. Bernard's Church. In the alley, things had changed, but he wouldn't look until he had walked deliberately down to the tenement.

He knew then she must have won. He put his face close to the wall and closed his eyes. The smell of hot baked stone was there, three-quarters of a century of hot summer afternoons and children's faces pressed against the wall, leaving a faint scent of bubble gum and candy and kid sweat. The building had stood through the exodus of middle-class white families and the influx of poor white families and minorities and the onslaught of urban renewal, waiting for Angie to come back and touch it one more time, touch it and make him really and truly IT. And now he was here, too, Milo was here, but grown big and not very afraid anymore, now that it was done. If he had to be IT, if he had no choice—and he'd never had, really—he would be a real IT, the biggest, the scariest, and no one would know until it was too late.

Counting to one hundred by fives hadn't taken very long at all

—not nearly as long as he had remembered. When he'd opened his eyes, he'd found the boy hanging around in front of the rented cottage.

"Hi," he'd said to the boy. "Know what I'm doing?"

"No, what?" the boy had asked.

"I'm looking for some friends." Milo had smiled. "I used to live here."

Now they stood at the end of the alley together and Milo smiled again to see that the house was still there. But then, he'd known that it would be. He walked slowly down Fourth to stand directly across the street from it, staring at the stubborn front door. It probably still wouldn't open. The red paint had long flaked away and been replaced by something colorless. What grass had surrounded the place had died off. Overhead the sky, almost as blue as it had been that day, was beginning to deepen. He listened for children's voices and the sound of the bigger boys' English bikes ticking by on the street. If he strained, he could almost hear them. It was awfully quiet today, but some days were like that, he remembered.

"Who lives there?" he asked the boy. "Who lives in that house now?"

"Nobody."

"Nobody? Nobody at all?"

"It's a dump." The boy bounced the heel of his right sneaker against the toe of his left. "I been in there," he added, with only a little bit of pride.

"Have you."

"Yeah. It's real stinky and dirty. Joey says it's haunted, but *I* never seen nothin'."

Milo pressed his index finger along his mouth, stifling the laugh that wanted to burst out of him. *Haunted? Of course it's haunted, you little monster—I've been haunting it myself!* "Must be fun to play in, huh?"

The boy looked up at him as though he were trying to decide whether he could trust Milo with that information. "Well, nobody's supposed to go in there anymore, but you can still get in."

Milo nodded. "I know. Say, did you ever play a game where

you have to put your feet in and somebody counts everybody out and the last one left is IT?"

The boy shrugged. "Like 'eenie, meenie, miney, mo?'"

"Something like that. Only we used to say it differently. I'll show you." Milo knelt again, putting the toe of his shoe opposite the boy's sneaker, ignoring the boy's bored sigh. Oh, yes, he'd show the boy. It wouldn't be nearly as boring as the boy would think, either. The boy was a Stevie. That meant that pretty soon there'd be a Sammy coming along and then maybe a Flora and a Bonnie and all the rest of the ones who had helped look for him and who had told Angie where to find him. But he'd give all of them a better chance than they'd given him. He'd do the chant for them, the way he was doing now for the boy, starting with the boy's foot first.

> *Eenie, meenie, ipsateenie*
> *Goo, gah, gahgoleenie*
> *Ahchee, pahchee, Liberaci*
> *Out goes Y-O-U!*

Milo grinned. "Looks like I'm IT." He stood up. Still IT, he should have said. They hadn't let him quit; they hadn't let him miss his turn. All right. He would take it now and keep taking it, because he was IT and it was his game now.

"C'mon," he said to the boy as he stepped off the curb to cross the street. "Let's see if that old house is still fun to play in."

*"If only I had done . . ." is the weary, often melancholy lament
of those who perceive their mistakes just a fraction too late to do
anything about them. It happens, of course, that once in a while
a second chance comes along to erase the "If only." It's not to be
counted on, and when it happens, the correction is not always
what our dreams would have it be. There are shadows in love as
well as in hate.*

*Peter Pautz lives and works as writer and photographer in
rural northwestern New Jersey. His work has appeared both here
in the United States and abroad—in Steve Jones and Dave Sut-
ton's excellent* Fantasy Tales.

COLD HEART

by Peter D. Pautz

The one thing that made Jeremy Ludlow happiest was that the
house had never sold. Each time he drove up the wide curving
private road, passed the discreet For Sale sign on the front gate,
he tried to imagine having to go somewhere else and a sharp
pang bit into his stomach, for he was not sure if Noreen would
have chosen another place. She may have just left him altogether. Somehow only in this place was she right; were they
right, he corrected himself. No demands, no clinging. Here they
engaged in not a mutual give-and-take but indulged in a taking, a
permitted selflessness, one from the other.

It was late fall, the trees having already shed almost every
crippled leaf that they would part with. The sun shot bright
streams against the smooth white stone, reflecting a rippling
pattern that looked like stucco from the boulevard but that became a moiré of gloss when you stood right next to the front wall
of the house. And only when you actually touched it could you
tell that it was glass-smooth. The only thing Jeremy had ever seen
like it was an altar stone in an old Catholic church. The marble
seemed glazed with a layer of frozen air that kept common flesh
at a respectable distance from the holy structure.

Again, Jeremy parked his car directly in front of the columned portico, quietly shutting the door as he stood looking up at the peaked roof, three stories above. Anywhere else it would have been a brazen act, a defiance to peering eyes. But here no one ever saw.

He walked slowly around the car and stood as if naked before the house. He rolled back his head, stretched his neck tightly, closed his eyes, and let the warmth of its loving presence caress him. With the wave of blessed emotion his mind drifted back. He could feel Noreen waiting patiently within, just as he'd felt her through his office door the minute before she had entered.

It was just less than a year before. Jeremy was carefully going over the final reports on the appraisals from the Whitney. No less than a half-dozen works by Frampton and DeMott had been sold in the last month by the prestigious Madison Avenue museum, and Concord-Ludlow had been called upon to provide fair-market values for tax purposes. It was a late Saturday afternoon and Jeremy Ludlow was alone in the office, his door closed. There had not been a sound, not even a smooth wind-shift of the tall building, yet something suddenly tightened the skin along the small of his back. In an instant he was sitting bolt upright, staring at his door. Crazy, he thought. I'm alone. Still, he watched the door for several breaths, never coming close to returning to his work, until the handle revolved and she stepped into the room.

She was tall, powerful in the manner of a long-distance runner. Her shoulder-length hair flicked lightly in a breeze he did not feel as she crossed the room and sat in the plush client's chair by his desk. He'd never remember her clothes. In his mind only the turquoise of her eyes enwrapped her.

In that handful of seconds he was hers, heart and soul. And body, he thought later.

"Mr. Ludlow." Her voice melded them, stripping away all his past. "Can you come to my house?"

He had to shake himself before he found the strength to answer. "I beg your pardon."

"Can you come to my house?"

I'd be delighted to, he wanted to say, but could only stare, his strength suddenly gone.

"I've some lovely old pieces I want to have cleaned," she continued. "And I want to insure them first. The bondsman requires an appraisal."

"Oh. Oh, of course," he stammered. "Would that be in Manhattan?"

"Goodness, no," she said. "Bergen County, just north of Woodcliff."

"And how soon would you be requiring the appraisal, Mrs. . . ." Even the discussion of business details could not bring him back safely to earth. His breath came in sharp, ecstatic gasps.

"Bradley. Noreen Bradley."

"Noreen Bradley," he said softly, intending to write it down, but he did not move. For she leaned gently forward and slid her hand lightly over his.

"Call me Noreen," she said, "please."

"Noreen," he whispered.

Then his phone rang. She took her hand back, and he wanted to cry. Heat flashed through him, and after a moment he snatched it from its cradle.

"What?" He was furious.

A pause at the other end of the line. "Honey, what's the matter?"

He forced a deep, calming shot of air into his lungs and spun his chair. He turned his back on the lovely creature before him and gazed out the window at the smoked granite across the street.

"Nothing," he said, "nothing. I'm sorry, Jan. What is it?"

"I just wanted to check and see if you'd be home by five o'clock. We've got that dance at the club tonight and you promised to take the kids shopping for their skis tonight, too."

"Oh, Christ. I'd completely forgotten." He frowned. How could he even care? "Look, I guess I'll be home by then. I've got a lot of work."

"Honey." She paused again, then went on sincerely to say, "I'm sorry if I've bothered you."

"No, I'm the one who's sorry." He smiled. Even after twelve years of marriage, her concern was as touching as ever. It was one of the reasons he knew they would last together. "I'll make sure I'm home by 5:30 at the latest, okay?"

"Sure."

"Okay, see you then. Love you."

"Love you, too."

He sighed heavily and turned back to his desk to hang up the telephone.

The magnificent lady—Noreen—was gone. His office door was wide open.

"Damn," he said sharply and slumped deeply into his chair.

Jeremy Ludlow did no more work that day. He arrived home at 8 P.M.

Two weeks later he had at least the blessing of hearing her voice again.

"Come to me," was all she said.

"Noreen?"

"Come to my house."

"When?" he said.

She did not answer.

"Where?"

She told him.

Then she was gone. The phone dead in his hand. He held it to his ear for a long time afterward, waiting for a sound of her gentle breathing, her strong, commanding heartbeat, but heard nothing.

Laying the phone carefully on his desk, he rolled down his sleeves, stood, and grabbed his coat.

In the outer office he quickly told his secretary, "Cancel all my appointments; I'll be gone the rest of the day," and ran to his car.

The drive out of Manhattan was infuriating. Every hunk of steel on the streets seemed to die in front of him, daring him to get out of his own car and rant and scream, delaying him all the more. Once out of the city he drove maniacally, dodging from one lane to the next around buses and tractor-trailers. The mass of entrance ramps in the Meadowlands fed further obstacles in front of him, but he bored his way through them, cursing, crying, fighting his way to a slower, gentler place. By the end there was more grass than asphalt, hundreds of trees for every building.

The house itself was set far back from the road. There was no brick wall surrounding the grounds, just an ironwork gate, but its sense of isolation bled the rest of the world away from him. The same way *her* voice robbed all others of their presence.

She was standing in the doorway when he pulled up. Her hair rustled in a breeze he could feel this time, though the two seemed out of sync somehow. He halted before climbing the stairs, waiting for a welcome, an invitation. Then he was close enough to look into her eyes and he came to her, followed her through a large vaulted foyer and into a sitting parlor.

Sunlight coursed through tall, glistening windows. To his mind the furnishings were as indistinct as her garb. Only she was real, touchable, he told himself as she once again took his hand in hers. Her hair was the only source of movement.

"You have a cold heart," her voice said in his heart.

"Not the way you make me feel." His was barely a whisper.

"Yes, cold." She hesitated and stared into his eyes again. "Not calculating, not unfeeling. Strong, stable."

He would have laughed had he been able.

"It takes much. It will take whatever is offered."

"Whatever is offered." His words sounded soft and leadened to his own ears.

"Take me," she said.

And he did. As she took him.

They'd gone on for months. Taking, one from the other. Every few days she would call and he would come, leaving business or family, and take from her.

But as the spring came their lovemaking had stopped. He still came when she called. In the front parlor where she'd first taken him, they would sit and talk as she prepared him for responsibilities and for love. Then they would walk the house, particularly on cloudy days, wandering the halls, never staying long near or in any room, returning always to the parlor. Even here he began to notice her discomfort, and slowly he began to insist that they continue their strolls.

When the lovemaking stopped, he tried for the first time to remember her body, to recall the ecstasy of their entwining, but could not. A few nights as they lay together, Jan noticed the wistful joy in his face and offered her own loving—didn't he used to call it that?—smile and beseeching hands, but he could only close his eyes and turn from her. She would stroke his back then and try to talk with him, but he remained cold and unresponsive.

Sometimes she had cried herself to sleep against his back while he tried in vain to recapture those precious moments with Noreen. He could no more describe her breasts than he could envision her walk or how her clothes draped. Indeed, in the interminable days and nights without her, he could not bring to his mind's eye anything about her except his craving need of her, of her presence. It did not surprise or distress him, however. For he had taken of her, as had she of him, and the desire was implicit.

Neither did it surprise or distress him when she vanished.

She had been calling him almost daily. Summer was trailing on, burning the city with great gasps of August.

His body blazed with the need of her, and for the first time he did not wait for her call. On a Saturday afternoon he had simply stepped from the deck chair by the club's pool, where Jan splashed happily with their children, collected his clothes but not bothering to change, and drove his car to her.

Unannounced, he followed the roads, the driveway, and climbed the stairs to the wide doorway where she was waiting for him. As always, she'd taken his hand and led him to their settee in the front parlor. Even their long tours of the house started this way.

This time, though, she remained seated. She did not meet his eyes for a long time, and he worried terribly that he'd done something wrong, that she'd not take from him, this time or ever again.

She said nothing. She did not move. Yet after a while she vanished, simply faded away while she held his hand, until she was finally and completely gone, then she let go.

Jeremy did not scream or move. He gazed blankly into the empty space that she had been. An hour later he drove back to his wife and children.

Jan was sitting on the couch when he entered. She was about to say something, but when he stepped into the light she ran to the front closet, pulled an afghan from its shelf, and threw it around him. It was only then that he realized that he was still dressed solely in his bathing trunks. He was shivering, a light shade of blue. And it was still 72 degrees out.

The next morning had been horrid. Jan wore an exhausted

expression, the kind usually reserved for long-suffering widows. This time she did not even have the strength to ask him where he had been. The red glazing around her eyes evinced that she had been awake all night.

Try as he might, Jeremy could not bring himself to talk to her. He doubted he would get a response anyway and cared not at all enough to try. She merely sat in the wicker chair in the corner of their bedroom, unmoving, until her children came in an hour later and climbed into her lap. Eventually her arms closed around them and she cried without a sound.

For three months now the situation had gotten worse, although Jeremy rarely noticed anything beyond his time with Noreen. She'd called him two days after she had vanished and their meetings had regained their usual glorifying vagueness. For a while Jan asked him for explanations, wept when he tried some obvious lie, and finally withdrew altogether from him and the world around her. Her only solace seemed to be the children. For long hours every day and evening she held them, cuddling and stroking them like she had not done since they were infants.

In those brief moments of emotional awareness of her that came over Jeremy, he was immensely pleased. Children always seemed to give new life to the old and the lonely. As things now stood, a new baby would be their only hope if Noreen left him. The thought pained him terribly, for somehow he could sense her increasing distance, as if she had taken what she truly needed from him long ago, at the beginning, and now only waited with him for some final outcome.

He felt as if soon she would be ready to give him back to Jan.

The feeling had grown until that morning. Noreen had called him again, for the first time in over a week.

"Come to me," she'd said. "Come, these are my last moments."

He'd fled his office in a panic, but the fear slowly ebbed away as he approached the house. She was not waiting for him this time; the door was shut, yet he could feel her inside, stronger, more full of life than ever before. As he climbed the stairs to the entrance, he noticed that the stonework seemed duller, its shine somewhat muted even in the bright sunlight. He had to press his shoulder against the door to pry it from the jamb. It opened stiffly.

The moment he entered, Noreen's voice came to him, hurrying him to the parlor. He raced to the settee, though she was not there. A sheet covered it. Whether it was new or not, he could not say. In the year he'd been coming to her he could not remember the color or design or texture of the settee. It could have been covered, he realized; until now it had never mattered. In a second the panic was back, squeezing his heart.

Then he heard her voice again.

"Jeremy, it's over," she said. He spun around, searching the room for her. She was not there.

"Noreen," he pleaded to the empty air. He crumpled to the settee, his face twitching in his hands, and wept. It felt as if his entire chest were being forced through his throat.

"I love you, Jeremy." It was the first time she had ever said it.

His voice was weak, muffled by his sobbing. "Stay with me," he begged.

"I can't, Jeremy," she said softly. "I must rejoin my family. I've been away too long."

He looked up imploringly at the deserted room but he could not speak.

"I'll always be with you, Jeremy." Her voice was fading, spreading thin and distant toward the walls. A moment later, as she vanished from him forever, she added, "I've left something for you, my love. Take it, and remember me."

She was gone.

The sun set before he could bring himself to rise, and when he did, incongruously, he sneezed. He wiped at his face, leaving a dark smudge of dust across his cheeks, and stared down at the settee. It was no longer empty. Lying before him on the dirty sheet was a bundle. He bent and inspected it carefully. Even through the pain he smiled. It would be all right now, he knew.

Delicately carrying the gift from Noreen, Jeremy left the house and drove home; to Jan, to reunite their family.

With a little love from him and a little acceptance from Jan, he knew it would all be perfect again. He could have the best of both worlds.

Except that when he gave Jan the package, she stared at him blankly. Gazing back at the empty blanket in her hands she started to ask him something, but when the light, gentle crying came, she dropped the precious bundle and began screaming.

*What do you do with devotion? With love? You can either accept
it gratefully, and with open arms, or you can harden your heart
and reject it. There's a third possibility—you can see it for what it
is and run for your life.*

*Jesse Osburn is an Oklahoman who makes his first print ap-
pearance here, with a story that came in late and one I couldn't
pass up.*

PEPPERMINT KISSES

by Jesse Osburn

"Hey you, Bronco. How about a kiss?"

Bronco skirted the canopied entrance of Mulford's Meat Market. The worn heels of his boots slipped on the rain-washed
sidewalk and left him standing with his back against a plate-glass
window and his feet spread at clumsy angles. He studied the door
of the market for movement but saw nothing beyond the
webbed pattern of green-and-silver lights.

"A kiss, Bronco. That's all I want."

The voice came from the darkest corner of the entrance.
Bronco pressed a grease-spotted package to his chest and took a
step forward.

"Give me a kiss, Bronco."

A breeze saturated his face and prodded his nostrils with
mixed scents of peppermint, salt water, and baked ham. Shadows
swirled past his line of vision and mixed with the heated colors of
a neon sign. The sidewalk seemed miles behind him. Bronco
swallowed a mouthful of warm saliva.

The lights surrounding the door were powdery gold and flut-
tered from side to side like the wings of a moth. An old man's face
became visible on the outer edges of the revolving lights.

"Mr. Mulford?" Bronco whispered. "That you, sir?"

The old man nodded. His eyes, rimmed with fire, were hol-
lowed blackness beyond the red. He stepped forward until mossy
shadows covered his face.

Mulford's fingers cupped Bronco's right ear and drew him

toward the entrance. Bronco hugged the package closer to his chest. The urge to follow the old man left him limp.

Mulford pointed to the package.

"What you have there, boy?"

"Food, sir." Bronco extended the parcel to the old man. "Food for Hoover and Tipper. You hungry, Mr. Mulford? I'll share."

"Hungry?" Mulford rested his chin against Bronco's shoulder. "I'm not hungry. I'd like a kiss though."

The old man's grip tightened on Bronco's ear. Mulford's lips, wide and bruised, were inches from his cheek.

The old man pressed closer and twisted his stomach into Bronco's belt buckle.

"I love you, Bronco."

Mulford's lips brushed his cheek.

Bronco stumbled back. The old man lunged forward, grabbed the package, and hurled it into the darkness of the entrance.

"Be a sweet boy. Give an old man a kiss. We'll find your friend Hoover. He'd like a kiss, too, I'll bet."

Mulford's breath was heavy against Bronco's face.

"Hoover. The food's for Hoover and it's gone. Poor Hoover. He'll starve."

"It's Tipper I'm worried about, Bronco." The sound of Hoover's voice playing in his memory shattered the night air. *"Tipper. She's so hungry."*

Sweat trailed from beneath Bronco's arm. Mulford's lips no longer felt soothing against his face. The old man's tongue flicked past his ear with the swarm of an angry fly and left double trails of congealed saliva on his cheek and lower lip.

He pinched both hands into the man's face until he felt his fingernails cut into flesh.

"Leave me alone."

Bronco shoved and the old man reeled back into darkness.

Bronco ran from the market. The steady clicking of his heels against the wet cement seemed to grow louder with each step. He wiped sweat from the back of his neck and brushed his hands down the legs of his faded denims.

The rain was heavier now that he was out from under the canopy of Mulford's Market. His hair was plastered in small ringlets across his forehead and drooped past his eyebrows. He felt Mulford's saliva burning his cheek.

He was blocks away from the old man when he stopped. He leaned against the marble column of Mid-City Savings & Loan and wiped his face with the sleeve of his shirt. The old man's saliva seemed to be spreading everywhere. His shirt was stained brown and reeked with the odor of peppermint and rotted ham. Bronco tore open the white pearl buttons and let rain drizzle down his chest.

From the darkened recesses of storefronts he heard whispers and moans.

"Kiss me. Please, give me a kiss."

Hoover's apartment building was nestled a block off Main Street. Bronco stepped inside the splintered door and rested his elbow on a stair railing. The threadbare carpet smelled moldy like the fur of a wet pup.

"Who's there?"

Bronco looked to the top of the stairs.

"It's me, Hoover."

"Food? You bring food, man?"

"No." Bronco's throat tightened. "Mulford's one of them now. He took what I had."

"Damn, Bronco. Tipper's got to eat."

"I know." His mouth tasted sour.

Hoover shifted and placed one hand on the wall.

"We found coffee in the basement. It's all we have." The boy slapped the wall. "You're welcome to it."

Upstairs Bronco pushed open the door to Hoover's apartment. The room was quiet and blocked with shadows. Bronco stood motionless and listened to the sounds of soft breathing.

"Hoover?"

"Over here, Bronco." Hoover struck a match on the planked floor and lit a candle. "Coffee's on the stove." Hoover turned to a bunk behind him and kicked at the mattress. "Tipper, bring Bronco some coffee, huh?"

Tipper stood and brushed matted curls of blond hair from her forehead. She smiled and attempted a curtsy. Her frail legs quivered as she moved to a far corner.

"Still bad out, huh?" Hoover asked.

Bronco nodded.

"I tried, Hoover. I had sandwiches, but . . ."

"Old Man Mulford took them. You said that already." Hoover leaned back in the cane-bottomed chair and closed his eyes.

"How's your mama, Hoover?"

"Bronco? That you, Bronco?"

The smell of peppermint brushed Bronco's face. He looked down at the bunk where Tipper had been earlier. Hoover's mother smiled up at him.

"Kiss me, Bronco."

The woman's face, like Mulford's, was moss-colored and her eyes rimmed fiery red. Her lips parted open enough to reveal a tongue split into two swollen sections.

"Kiss me, Bronco. You, too, Hoover."

Hoover kicked the bed frame.

"Go to sleep, Mama."

"All I want is a kiss. Give your sweet mama a kiss." She tried to sit but her wrists and ankles were bound by tattered remnants of a floral tablecloth.

"Here's your coffee, Bronco." Tipper held the mug toward him. She curtsied and her knees shifted unsteadily.

"Thanks," Bronco said.

"You should have brought Mr. Mulford here, Bronco. He's nice. He gives me candy sometimes."

The girl returned to the bunk and sat near her mother's shoulders.

"I like Mr. Mulford," she said. "You should have brought him here."

Bronco eased into a wooden chair near the wall and sipped at the mug. Grains of coffee stuck to his tongue and forced their way past his throat.

"Sleep here tonight, Bronco," Hoover said. He took a blanket from beside the sofa and spread it across the floor. "Tipper sleeps on the sofa. Tomorrow we'll find something to eat." Hoover snuffed the candle. "Stay away from Mama. She's always worse at night."

Tipper moved from the bed and stretched out on the sofa. She looked even thinner in the dim light. Her blue gown clung to her buttocks and outlined the shape of her protruding ribs.

Hoover checked the knots that bound his mother, then sat cross-legged on the floor with his spine pressed against the foot of the bed.

Bronco sipped at the coffee and tilted his chair against the wall.

Hoover's mother twisted her arms and legs. She lolled her head to one side and smiled.

"Kiss me, Bronco."

Bronco could hear Tipper's stomach roll with the sound of hunger.

He tasted the coffee and closed his eyes.

Hours later he awakened with a jolt.

Hoover stood in front of the chair with one hand on Bronco's shoulder.

"It's Mama."

Bronco glanced to the opposite side of the room. The woman lay on the bunk, covered with the blanket.

"She's always worse at night," Hoover said. "She almost kissed me. I held a pillow over her face."

Bronco tried to stand but Hoover pushed him down.

"I don't want Tipper to see. You look after her until I get back, huh?"

Hoover gathered the woman in his arms and carried her to the door.

Bronco looked to the sofa. Tipper rolled to her back and rubbed her eyes.

The door closed. Bronco breathed deep and listened to Hoover's heavy footsteps descend the stairs.

Tipper sat up and wrapped her arms around her stomach.

"Where's Hoover going?"

"Go back to sleep," Bronco answered. "Hoover'll be back. Then we'll get something to eat."

"Mama kissed Hoover, huh, Bronco?"

"No, Tipper."

"She wants to kiss Hoover, though, don't she?"

Bronco nodded.

Tipper pulled her legs beneath her and braced her hands on the cushions.

"What's it like to be kissed, Bronco?"

"Good. Sometimes."

Tipper pushed hair from her forehead.

"I asked Hoover to kiss me so I'd know what it's like. He says it isn't right, a brother kissing his sister." Her eyes filled with tears. "Would you kiss me, Bronco? Just so I'll know."

She stood and moved toward the chair.

"It's not right," Bronco said. "You're a baby, Tipper. I can't kiss a baby."

"Kiss me, Bronco. Just so I'll know."

He brushed tears from the girl's face with his thumbs.

Tipper leaned forward and pressed her nose against his cheek.

Bronco closed his eyes and touched his lips to the girl's mouth.

Bronco rocked back and forth in the chair. He scraped his boot heels across the floor. The room was quiet, too quiet.

"What's keeping Hoover, do you think? He's been gone for hours."

He looked across the room. Tipper was asleep.

His stomach burned. He belched and the taste of coffee coated his tongue. Bronco licked his upper lip and tasted another flavor, a sweetness he didn't remember from before.

Footsteps sounded in the hallway. The doorknob rattled. Bronco stood and brushed his hands down the legs of his denims.

Hoover stepped inside the apartment and leaned against the wall.

"Bronco? Everything all right?" The boy wiped sweat from his forehead. "Mama wasn't dead, Bronco. She woke up and all she talked about was how I should be more like Tipper. Tipper was sitting by Mama on the bed and I turned my back once. I thought Tipper might have . . ."

"Don't worry none," Bronco said. "Tipper's a good kid. She worried about Mr. Mulford, though. She insisted I go find him."

Bronco nodded toward the sofa.

Hoover looked across the room. His face paled.

The girl and the old man were sitting side by side, asleep. Tipper shifted and nestled her head closer to Mulford's arm.

"She wants to find your mama, Hoover." Bronco belched again. His mouth tasted sweet, like peppermint.

Hoover'd like the way his mouth tasted, he thought. Hell, everybody likes peppermint.

He took a step toward the other boy.

"Let's go find your mama, Hoover." Bronco flicked one section of his tongue across his lips. "But first, come give your old buddy Bronco a kiss."

Reality supposedly exists just outside the window, out there in the streets where people have to struggle even in their sleep for survival. Liberals would have us clean the streets up and help those who can't help themselves; conservatives don't deny that help is needed, but they move more slowly; and a few say that such conditions are a fact of Nature and can't be helped at all. Nature, however, is never as Benevolent as the romantics (or anyone else, for that matter) would have it.

J. Michael Straczynski lives and works in California, and has a deft hand with shadows, especially those making noises on the other side of the door.

A LAST TESTAMENT FOR NICK AND THE TROOPER

by J. Michael Straczynski

Nick checked his watch. He pushed a button, and 1:45 flashed on the liquid crystal display, alternating with day, date, and seconds. By pushing another button, he could set the watch to chime every hour on the hour, backlight the display, and tell him what time it was somewhere else, in another time zone. Not that he knew where somewhere else *was*, though. There hadn't been time to find out from the old guy he'd taken it from. The geezer had fought like hell to keep it, with good reason. The piece had to be worth at least sixty, maybe even eighty bucks, enough for that new set of Italian blades Nick had had his eye on for nearly a week. But Nick wasn't going to sell it—at least not until he'd figured out where *somewhere else* was. Nick liked to figure out stuff like that.

Sooner or later he *would* figure it out. But not now. This wasn't the right time.

The time was 1:50. Ten minutes until Levin hit the street.

"Hey, Doc," Trooper said, "are we waiting for a bus or something?" He laughed at his own joke, sitting three steps below Nick on the tenement's concrete steps. Nick didn't bother to respond. It was too damn hot, and besides, Trooper knew what they were waiting for. The whole *block* knew you could set your watch by old man Levin. Every Monday and Friday, at exactly two o'clock, he hobbled down the four flights of stairs from his apartment across the street, crossed to the bank half a block away, withdrew some money, and picked up his supplies for the next few days at Lillian's Market on the corner. The routine was always the same. He rarely spoke to anyone, except the bank teller and sometimes Lillian, and he never carried more than one bag of groceries back to his apartment at a time. He wasn't a very strong man.

Which Nick did not find at *all* unfortunate.

For the third time in as many hours, Trooper untied and re-laced his heavy leather boots, pulling the laces as tight as he could before tying them off. He inspected the boots carefully, brushing away a speck of dust here, rubbing at a scuff over there with a moistened thumb. Trooper always had to be doing *something* with his hands, and most times it had something to do with taking care of his boots, his prized possessions. It was a habit Nick found distracting, clear evidence of an undisciplined mind.

"So what's the plan, Doc?" Trooper asked, stretching his feet out toward the sidewalk, where they caught and held the sunlight. "I mean, stealing some old guy's box of Twinkies ain't my style, y'know?"

"If you don't want a cut off this, you don't *have* to stay," Nick said. "Nobody's making you stick around. I can take care of this on my own if you're not interested." Briefly, Nick almost wished he *would* leave. He also wished Trooper would talk less and think more. But Nick was too smart to put much stock in wishes.

"Okay," Trooper said, raising his hands, "I was just asking a question. Don't get tense." He flashed a lopsided grin. *Don't get tense* was a private joke. Whenever Nick got mad at someone—getting *intense,* he called it—he'd leaf through the copy of *Gray's Anatomy* he'd liberated from the library, having once seen a poster that said *Reading Changes Lives,* and refresh his memory of the most vulnerably positioned arteries. Nick was one danger-ous person with a blade, of which he had many collections. He was also very fast, and very quiet when he worked. As a result, to Trooper and a few others, he was Doc. To the rest, he was Nick or Sir, but never anything else. At least, never more than once.

Nick checked his watch again. It was 1:56. "Let me ask you a question," Nick said. "Being that Levin's a foreigner, he don't get Social Security or retirement or anything like that, right?"

"Right," Trooper said.

"And he never goes to the bank on Tuesdays like all the rest when their welfare checks come in, right?"

"Again right."

"So what does that tell you?" Nick asked, closing and opening his latest acquisition, a six-inch imported stiletto with a pearl handle and engraved shaft.

A minute slipped by. Trooper considered the question, scratched at his week-old beard, and finally shrugged. "I don't know," he said, grinning broadly, "what?"

Nick glanced up and down the street as if Trooper wasn't there, then shook his head. Sometimes he wondered why he bothered. "It tells you that when Levin came over from wherever he used to live—"

"Israel," Trooper said. "I stopped by Lillian's a coupla days ago for some cigarettes and heard her tell somebody he's from Israel."

"Okay, Israel then," Nick said. "That's not important. What *is* important is that he must've brought along some money, money that he's been living on all this time, right?"

"Sure," Trooper said, "I guess so. But what good does that do us? It's all in the bank, except for the few bucks he takes out to buy food with, and that ain't worth the hassle. Just a waste of time, when we could be doin' other things." He reached into his shirt pocket and pulled out a plastic baggie. "You wanna get stoned?"

"Keep it," Nick snapped. He didn't believe in getting stoned during working hours. It was a sign of weakness, and muddied up the mind. "Look, it's simple. *A*, we know Levin's got money, probably a lot of it, and *B*, all we ever *see* him buy with it is food. But I hear he's got all *kinds* of goodies stashed away in his place— jewelry, rings, silver, even some coins from all over the world. It's all locked away up there, not doing *anybody* any good. At least, not yet. You follow?"

Trooper smiled, nodded. This time he understood *perfectly*.

At the base of a faded brownstone across the street, a door

opened, its black paint covered with initials and obscenities roughly carved into the wood beneath. Through the door stepped a man in a long black overcoat and black hat, both frayed with age. A beard cascaded down over his chest, and two ends of a prayer shawl waved at the bottom of his coat as he stepped slowly and carefully down the steps, onto the sidewalk, and across the street.

Nick checked his watch. "Two o'clock," he said.

The fire escape was a lot shakier than Nick had anticipated. It was a wonder that the whole thing hadn't collapsed years ago. But it got him to the fourth-floor window facing into Levin's apartment, and that was sufficient. Even so, the climb had taken nearly five minutes, and he knew that Levin's errands never required more than twenty minutes.

But that was all right by Nick. He'd only come for the tour in the first place. Besides, the Trooper was following Levin on his rounds to see what else he could learn, and would signal Nick as soon as the old man entered the building. No sweat.

Nick squinted through the soot-grimed window, careful not to disturb the layers of city grit. He wasn't sure what he was looking for, but he was certain he'd recognize it when he saw it.

But the sun's angle was all wrong, so that most of the apartment was lost in shadow. What he could see was spare and, Nick decided, surprisingly uncluttered for the home of an old man. Directly in front of him was the kitchen, containing two straight-backed chairs and a formica table checked in patterns of grey and white. Of the living room beyond, Nick could only make out a chair, a faded brown couch that sagged in the middle, a lamp, and a pair of high cabinets. Lace curtains hung from the living room windows, the shades behind them barely admitting a thin shaft of sunlight.

Just as Nick's eyes were getting used to the dim light inside the apartment, the door opened and Levin stepped inside, closing the door again behind him. Cursing silently under his breath, Nick dropped down beneath the window, out of sight. He checked his watch. Levin was back a full twelve minutes early. There had been no warning, and there was no sign of the Trooper in the alley beneath him.

Nick eased himself back down the fire escape ladder, freezing with every shake and rattle of the structure, possibilities and explanations running through his mind. What if the Trooper had been caught? Or if he'd done something stupid? Or if he'd decided to split, or rip Levin off for the few dollars he took from the bank and *then* split.

Seconds after Nick leapt from the last rung of the ladder to the glass-spattered alley, Trooper turned the corner and came up beside him, grinning that same sloppy grin. "Sorry I'm late," he said.

Furious, Nick grabbed him by the front of his shirt. "Where the *hell* were you?" he hissed, his nose only a few inches from Trooper's. "I could've got nailed up there, you stupid creep. *Then* where'd we be?" He pushed the Trooper away and stalked out of the alley.

"Hey, look, I *said* I was sorry, man," Trooper said, catching up and walking quickly to stay alongside Nick. "Besides," he said, breathing hard, "you haven't let me tell you *why* I was late."

Nick stopped, turned, faced him. "Okay," he said, "I'm listening. So talk."

Trooper took a second to catch his breath and collect his thoughts, and began. "Just like you said, I followed Levin out to the bank. When he got inside, there wasn't anybody else in line, so he got to go right up to the window. Only *this* time, instead of handing the teller a check, he pulled out one of those savings account books, you know."

"A passbook."

"Right. Anyway, he says something to the teller, and she goes back to check with somebody else behind one of those desks. Then she comes back with some dude in a suit, and *he* talks to Levin for a coupla minutes. I tried to hear what they was saying, but I was too far away. Next thing I know, Levin and the guy in the suit sign some piece of paper, and the teller starts countin' out a bunch of money."

"How much money?" Nick asked. Trooper had definitely succeeded in getting his attention.

"A *lot*," Trooper said, pleased. It wasn't often that Nick let him talk for a long time without interrupting or telling him how dumb he was. "It looked like the old man damn near cleaned out his whole life savings. Then he went over to a table, stuck something in an envelope, closed it, and walked out of the bank. I thought maybe we could take him before he got back to his place, but there were too many cops around, parked over by Lillian's. I figured that'd be his next stop, but instead he headed back to the apartment."

"So why didn't you signal me?"

"I'm gettin' to that. Anyway, he goes inside the hallway, and from the street I see him put the envelope in his mailbox and lock it. Now, I figured the money was in the envelope. Old duffers like that are *always* being stupid and sending money in the mail. So as soon as he went upstairs, I tried to get the box open, but couldn't swing it. That's when I came after you."

Nick nodded, considering it. It was a good thing he *hadn't* been able to open the mailbox. If he had, Nick knew he'd never have seen the Trooper or the money. Like always, Trooper proved he couldn't handle *anything* on his own. "C'mon," Nick said, heading back the way they'd come. "Looks like we're going to have a Special Delivery of our own."

Picking the mailbox lock, set alongside the rest in a metal row along one side of the empty hall, took three minutes and the tip of Nick's new stiletto, sacrificed for a just cause. When he removed the envelope, Nick found it disappointingly slim. He shot a disgusted glance in Trooper's direction, closed the box, and headed out, jaw set tight in frustration. Trooper shrugged and followed, keeping a few paces behind him, giving Nick plenty of room.

When things weren't going his way, Nick did *not* like to be crowded.

Hunkered down against the liquor store wall, Trooper bit into another Mars bar. "Well," he said out of the corner of his mouth, "what's in the letter?"

"I'm not sure," Nick said. "Give me a minute." Turning the page, he read the letter over for the second time, hoping to make more sense out of it this time around.

"My dear David," the letter read, "by the time you receive this, I will have left the country. Whether or not I shall return, I do not know. I write this so that you will not worry and so that you will understand. I must go because Reb Jeshia has died. What this has to do with my decision is hard to explain, but I must try.

"Five years ago, Reb Jeshia went to Israel, chasing legends. A silly occupation for a grown man, I thought, and told him so at the time. But Reb Jeshia was never one to be talked out of something once he took it into his head to do something. This time he had managed to convince himself that the eleventh jar of the plague still existed, if it ever had *really* existed in the first place.

"But I get ahead of myself. You see, David, when the Pharaoh would not let our people go, that we might serve God as He asked us to, it was said that God gave Moses eleven jars, all made by His hand. Each jar contained a terrible curse, each more terrible than the one before it. One by one Moses broke the seal on the jars, and Egypt was cursed. Its rivers and streams ran with blood, and the land itself was stricken. There were plagues of frogs, gnats, flies, boils, hail, locusts, and darkness. All the Egyptians' cattle were cursed and died. Finally there came the death of the firstborns, and the Pharaoh at last relented. When the people of Israel were freed, Moses was charged to keep the final jar, that it should be released if ever the people of Israel were threatened.

"With the death of Moses, the jar was given over to Aaron, then passed on from one generation to the next, its existence unknown to any but a few. Then the jar of the eleventh plague vanished, buried by its guardians when they were attacked by thieves in the desert. The jar remained lost for more than two thousand years, and the people of Israel, now defenseless, were scattered.

"Reb Jeshia first heard the legend from a rabbi while we were both interned at Treblinka. He believed that the jar had been intended by God to prevent the Holocaust, and swore that if he survived the camps, he would find the jar and guarantee that the Holocaust would never happen again. It was this dream alone that kept him alive through those terrible years.

"After the war, Reb Jeshia had a hard time saving the money for a private expedition, and for many years it was difficult to get into Israel at all, and many sections were too dangerous to enter. But at last he *did* leave, he did get his expedition, and after a year of digging, he did find the jar.

"At first, he intended to turn the jar over to the Israeli authorities. But he saw what was happening in the Middle East. Tempers were short, the government unstable. He was afraid of what might happen if he turned it over to the government, and even more afraid that news of its discovery would leak out to the wrong people. So he flew back to America long enough to turn the jar over to me, to hold it until he called for it.

"Two years ago, Reb Jeshia disappeared. So I waited. Finally, this week I received a telegram from my cousin in Tel Aviv. They found what was left of Reb Jeshia in a shallow grave just outside Haifa. There were two bullet wounds in his head. The government blamed it on Arab terrorists.

"But now the jar must go back to Israel, into the hands of someone wise enough to know what to do with it. I have a name, given me by Reb Jeshia, to be contacted only in the event of his death. So I *must* go, David. I do not know what plague the sealed jar contains. I only know that each plague was worse than the one preceding it, and since the tenth plague was the death of the firstborn, the next must be worse than even death itself. To be honest, neither do I know if the jar is even the *right* one. I only know that I owe it to Reb Jeshia to follow his last request. So today I have taken three thousand dollars from my savings. Tomorrow I shall take the first El Al to Jerusalem. I have told my landlord that I shall be gone for as much as a week or more. He said he will keep an eye on my apartment, so you needn't worry about it, or me. If I can, I will try to write you when I arrive. Please give my love to Sara and little Rachel. Shalom."

Nick flipped through the letter a last time, scanning the pages. A lot of it still didn't make much sense. Legends were just stories, like Jack and the Beanstalk or Mother Goose. But three thousand dollars . . . *that* was something Nick could understand. And with the landlord told that Levin would be out of town for a while, nobody'd even notice if the old duffer didn't show up for a while. It was the perfect setup.

Turning to the last page, he let his gaze drop to the final paragraph. *Worse than death itself.* He considered the idea for a moment, turning it in his mind like an unknown jewel. What could be worse than death, he wondered?

"Well?" Trooper asked, crushing the candy wrapper and tossing it into the street. "What's the story? What're we gonna do next?"

Nick stuffed the letter into his shirt pocket and stood up. "Next," Nick said, "we make ourselves a *lot* of money."

Trooper smiled.

According to Nick's watch, it was 11:17 and 52 seconds when Trooper finally met him in the alley behind Levin's apartment. He was supposed to have arrived at eleven sharp, which to Nick's mind was bad enough to start with. But even in the dim glow of a street lamp, he had little trouble figuring out how the Trooper had spent the last few hours.

"It was just one lousy, freakin' joint," Trooper said defensively. "Well, okay, maybe it was two. But it's okay, man. Really. I can handle it. Now c'mon; let's go."

Nick hesitated. This would complicate matters considerably. But there wasn't time to come back later, and he needed a backup man in case something went sour. It was now or never. "All right," Nick said, and started toward the fire escape. He had been quietly reevaluating his partnership with Trooper for some time, and this only further helped him realize that he might soon have to terminate the arrangement—permanently. Nick's first rule was to never leave any old partners for the cops to talk to, and Nick was nothing if not efficient at keeping rules. His rules, that is.

Reaching the fire escape, Nick turned his attention to climbing the cold steel ladder, which was slick with dew. He'd consider Trooper's "accident" later.

Climbing the slippery fire escape, the rungs barely visible in the darkness, took twice the usual time, hampered further by Trooper hanging back, climbing unsteadily. When they reached the fourth-floor landing, Trooper sat down heavily on the top step, back to the railing. The entire structure weaved slightly, and Nick cursed silently under his breath at the noise. When the fire escape had stopped vibrating, Nick crawled across the landing toward the window, straightening by degrees until he could just see inside.

Levin was sitting on the living room sofa, an open suitcase piled with clothes propped up on the coffee table. One by one, he picked up the remaining clothes beside him on the couch, folded them, and placed them in the suitcase, pausing now and again to rub at his eyes. Must be way past the old duffer's bedtime, Nick decided. Good. That meant they wouldn't have long to wait.

When as many clothes as could fit had been transferred, Levin shut the suitcase, fastened the locks and straps, and leaned back on the sofa, closing his eyes for a moment. Nick briefly wondered if Levin had at last gone to sleep. But then Levin sat up with a start, rubbed at his neck, then walked over toward a corner cabinet.

Trooper shifted position restlessly on the fire escape, causing the whole structure to sway slightly. Nick shot him a look, but Trooper was looking away, toward the freeway, where long ribbons of cars scissored their way through the darkness. Nick nudged him with his toe. Trooper mumbled something, nodded, but kept staring.

Returning his attention to the scene beyond the window, Nick saw Levin remove a wooden box from the cabinet, then walk back to the sofa. Nick squinted through the glass, trying for a better angle as Levin slid back a panel on the box, opened it, and removed a delicate-looking jar, wide at the bottom, narrowing into a fluted tube capped with red sealing wax. A pair of curved handles extended from either side. Even through the sooty window, Nick noticed the way the jar caught and held the light. It wasn't very long, just over a foot, and it looked old. Very old.

Flexing his arm, stiff from the moist night air, Nick watched as Levin pressed the jar to his chest. There was something on the old man's face that he could almost, but not quite, grasp. He decided that it probably wasn't worth the effort anyway and turned toward Trooper, still curled up beside the stairwell, still lost in his own personal fog. Nick exhaled slowly. This was definitely the last job he'd share with Trooper.

Just then Nick heard a sound, a soft, murmuring sound that came from inside the apartment. He turned to see Levin rocking gently back and forth, the box—with the jar once more inside—open on his lap. He was chanting a song that Nick had sometimes heard while hanging out in front of the synagogue over on Fifth Street. After a few minutes the chanting stopped and, still sitting on the sofa, Levin slept.

That was all Nick needed. Now he could settle down to business, he decided, allowing himself a brief smile of anticipation.

He knew how to take care of sleeping old folks. It was certainly a hell of a lot neater and a lot less trouble than running them down.

He nudged Trooper, motioning toward the window. Trooper nodded vaguely, trying unsteadily to rise to his feet as the fire escape swayed suddenly to the left, catching him off-balance. Arms flailing, he grabbed for the railing and missed.

"Oh, jeez," Trooper whispered, falling backward, poised motionless for the briefest second like a backstroking swimmer. Then the second passed, and he tumbled over the edge of the fire escape and down. It was to his credit, Nick noted, that his brief, near-silent exclamation was the only noise Trooper made during his four-story flight. It was the only thing he'd done right all evening.

Concerned that Trooper might make some noise *after* his fall that would bring the cops down on both of them, Nick scampered quickly but carefully down the fire escape, ready to finish off what fate had begun. But when he reached Trooper's side, he found that he no longer needed to worry about Trooper making any noise.

Trooper was dead, his neck twisted around at an impossible angle. Nick shrugged. It was just as well. Besides, it saved him the trouble of having to create an accident of his own later. No lights had gone on in or around the alley, so the drop probably went unnoticed. Even if it hadn't, nobody in this neighborhood would want to get involved anyway. Reassured, he started back up the fire escape. He had work to do.

Upon returning to Levin's window, he found the old man still asleep on the couch. He smiled grimly as he opened the knife he had chosen especially for this job—razor sharp, long, without a burr or nick anywhere on the blade. This was going to be easier than he'd thought.

Swimming up from a dream, Levin stirred, opened his eyes a crack, and idly wondered how he'd forgotten to close the kitchen window. Then he remembered that he hadn't opened it. Still groggy, he seemed to notice something bright and shiny swooping down toward him. He blinked.

That was the only thing he had time to do, and it was the last thing. Nick could find the carotid artery in his sleep, and like any good doctor, he was fast. A single, rapid pull of the blade, a clean incision, and it was all over. Levin had never actually done anything to offend him, so Nick made sure it was all quick and relatively painless. No sweat.

Wiping the knife off against the couch, Nick returned the blade to its sheath on his belt and started going through Levin's clothes. He came across a thick envelope in Levin's jacket, pulled it out, and riffled through the contents. Easily three grand, maybe a little more. Not bad for a night's work.

He checked his watch. It was 12:10. He knew he'd better get going, just in case somebody found Trooper's body and started raising hell. He glanced around quickly, looking for anything else of value. But the apartment was just about bare. Not even a television. No loss, he decided as he turned back toward the window.

Except . . .

Nick picked up the box from where it had fallen beside Levin on the couch. The lid was still open, revealing an inner layer of thick iron stained and discolored by the passage of years. He removed the jar, pausing to shake the box in case something else had been left inside. Finding nothing, he tossed the box back onto the couch and turned his attention to the jar.

It didn't look like much, but if it was even half as old as Levin thought, he figured he could probably pick up a few bucks for it somewhere. He turned it slowly, examining it from all sides. Although the walls of the jar were thick, and deeply etched with letters and figures he didn't recognize, he was surprised at how light it was, almost as if it was made of something more delicate than eggshells, almost like the fragile glass ornaments his father used to hang at Christmas. It felt strange in his hands, as if it were warm and cool, moist and dry, rough and smooth, growing and shrinking, all at the same time. When the light caught it at just the right angle, the jar glimmered with subtle colors that flowed faintly beneath the surface, colors that Nick couldn't quite name. He shook it. Nothing rattled inside. He tried to remember what else Levin's letter had said about it, but none of it made any sense. Just the ramblings of an old man. There was one thing he remembered, though, one question that had preyed and was still preying on Nick's curiosity as he poked at the wax seal at the end of the jar's fluted neck: What *was* worse than death itself?

And what, he wondered, was on the other side of that seal?

Abruptly, with a final prod, the seal vanished with a puff of stale air.

For a moment nothing happened. Or, more precisely, *nothing was happening*. The air in the room hung heavy, the sounds of the street below grew muffled, then faded, the clock on the wall stopped ticking, and Nick found himself holding his breath, waiting for . . . what?

Suddenly a patch of darkness formed in the room, spinning slowly, then faster, scattering papers, books, and furniture. Nick tried to look at it, but somehow his eyes couldn't quite seem to focus on it, to take it all in, as if it was somehow farther away than it seemed. He stepped back, shielding his eyes as the room dimmed, as the light itself was absorbed, tumbling crazily into the darkness. Then everything was black, an absolute night that only existed somewhere else, where no stars had ever shone.

A wind whipped up from nowhere, everywhere, blowing through the walls from across lands that were without name. To Nick it was a wind the smell of dust, of books left long unopened, of burning incense, of mold, of dry leaves, of rusting iron and rotting wood, of moist clay and dried blood, of fire and ash, of decaying seaweed and yellowed flesh. It was a wind the sound of distant thunder nearing, of muffled screams, of hideous laughter, of babies crying, of pounding drums, of muttered whispers and a Voice that called out in a language that had existed before there were words.

And there was the fear. Thrown to the floor, Nick lay gasping for air, eyes clamped shut, genuinely and mortally afraid for the first time in his life. Small noises came from the back of his throat. Had he known how, he might have prayed. Not that it would have done any good, there in the thing that was not night but something older. It was too late, Nick knew, even for prayer.

Then as suddenly as it had appeared, the wind vanished and the sounds diminished, though the room was still held in absolute darkness. There was an utter stillness and a sense of breathless apprehension, of waiting for . . . *something*.

Curled up on the floor in a fetal ball, Nick lay shivering, surrounded by night, asking himself the same question over and over, hysterically, desperately, the answer more urgent now than before: *What was worse than death?*

Then Nick heard it. The new sound. First soft, distant, then louder, coming with the thud and scrape of heavy boots on the fire escape stairs. Nick tried to scream, but nothing emerged. There was only *the* sound, now just outside the window, moving closer.

Trooper was calling his name.

There are times when accepting guilt for a sin of commission is a lot easier than accepting guilt for something you wish you had done and didn't have the courage to do. There are also times when denying guilt doesn't do you the least bit of good.

Melissa Mia Hall is a poet, photographer, and short story writer from Texas; her work has appeared in Shayol, The Twilight Zone, *and others. She is not nearly as gentle as she appears.*

MARIANA

by Melissa Mia Hall

Her face is a moon in the room, balefully white, luminous. He walks toward her gently, a wind in the twilight, barely moving. At the open window, curtains blow forward, touching her cheek. He stands over her. She looks up at him, darkness in her eyes. He trembles. Her neck arches like a swan's. She starts to say something. He bends closer, as if to hear better. She lies back, sighing, her hair branchlike across the bedspread. He takes the pillow with the crocheted edging and presses it against her face. She struggles faintly and then surrenders. He removes the pillow with the rough indention of that face and stares at it.

He goes to the chair by the other window and sits. The dusk has faded. The night has come. A breeze throws a curtain against one cheek and he shivers as she did earlier. Cloth against skin. He is naked and needs to put on his clothes. He needs to leave. He thinks of all the fingerprints he has left in this room the last two years. The air's cold. He stands and looks for his clothes. He assembles himself, each bit of clothing an extension of himself. Afterward he covers her with a quilt. As he straightens up, he catches his reflection in the mirror on her closet door. It's a dim image, mysterious and questioning. He waves; the image waves.

As he leaves, he stubs his foot against the telephone table. He thinks about calling the police but decides he would rather go eat somewhere.

He locks her house carefully. He has left her bedroom windows

open. When her body begins to putrefy, the room will need air.
And he wants someone to find her quickly.

The traffic's not bad. He admires his hands on the wheel. Such
strong, graceful, capable hands.

A car darts out from a side street. He throws on the brakes and
screams, but there's no accident. He makes it to Luigi's safely.

He orders veal parmigiana and plays with the tomato sauce,
picks at the cheese. It tastes good but his appetite leaves something to be desired. He sips at his red wine and gazes at the
empty booth next to him. Mariana is dead. Byron has killed her.
He swirls the wine. His fingers clench the stem too tightly. The
glass breaks. The wine ruins the red-checked tablecloth and
forms a pool in his veal. A waiter rushes to his booth, solicitous
and grave. Byron has cut his thumb. Mariana loved Italian food,
authentic and inspired imitations alike.

"You're hurt—let me see—"

"It's nothing." Byron winds a napkin around his thumb.

The waiter looks terribly concerned, almost suspicious.

"We have Band-Aids. You really ought to let us see to it."

"No, it's okay, really."

"Would you like some more wine? And I'm afraid your food's
spoiled. We can—"

He gestures wildly, "No, I'm not hungry. Just let me pay the
bill."

"But there's no charge," the waiter says in his clipped nasal
tone. He glances at the cashier, who's also the wife of the owner.
She nods cryptically.

Byron gets up to leave, watching them both cautiously.

"Thank you."

"Please come back."

They act like they don't remember the times they used to
come, holding hands and laughing—Byron and Mariana, Mariana
and Byron—

When he gets home, the police are not waiting for him. Everything is very quiet. His cat, Roosevelt, purrs around his legs and
rubs hello. His phone mate blinks warmly. Messages.

He listens to the playback. Nothing urgent.

He goes to the kitchen to feed Roosevelt and find himself some
cookies. In the living room he rummages in the cabinet for his

photo albums, his many photographs of Mariana. He holds them in his lap and wonders what he should do. He could burn them, tear them into tiny bits, or throw them as they are into the dumpster out behind the apartments. Maybe they could be construed as evidence. He's not certain, but they must be incriminating. He lifts one particularly lovely portrait up to the light, reflecting on the moment of its inception.

"Like this?"

"One, two, three—look to your left—think of something wonderful—me, of course. That's it! Laugh at me—love me—love me—"

"Byron!"

"Yeah—"

"Lord!"

The picture was of Mariana in a white sundress sitting on a stump. A redwood stump. And the brothers and sisters of that tree swung high around her.

Byron sets the pictures down and wanders around the room looking for his camera. It's on the bookshelf. He studies the film counter. One roll left. He turns to the right, and her face on the wall smiles.

He's not even a professional photographer. He is—he is—thoughts stream away from him. He knocks the camera off the shelf. It falls face down on the carpet. He is a drama teacher, a sometime actor who never had the courage to leave the campus. He is a sometime writer who never had the courage to send a story to a magazine or finish the third chapter of a book or the second act of a play. But now he is a murderer.

The cat screams, shoots across the room, a grey rocket. Byron jumps, wheels around, working his mouth for his own scream and is only able to rouse a raspy "Wha-at?"

Roosevelt crouches in the middle of a half-full bookshelf, hair on end, tail straight as a telephone pole. He hisses and snarls.

A timid knocking upon the door. He tells the cat to calm down and opens the door without consulting the peephole. The fear has made him oddly bold.

No one is there. Byron waits for a few minutes, then closes the door and locks it. Maybe he should call the police. Maybe he should go to bed.

He cries to himself as he readies for bed. He deserves the electric chair. Tomorrow he'll turn the last roll into the photo lab for immediate development and then maybe he'll turn himself in to the police.

Byron crosses himself and prays to his guardian angel like he used to do growing up in New Jersey. Then he stares at the ceiling.

Auburn hair trying to be chestnut, a straight nose with a softness at the tip, her mouth like a rosebud fading in the sun, grey eyes set apart by that space so gentle, so kissable, the piquant oval of that countenance, the perfect forehead, the point of her chin, the ivory fairness that carried only a faint dusting of freckles, the cameo of her face—

Flat on his back, he imagines what she looked like that first time. She was blinking in a torrential rain, hair plastered back. He ran into her in front of the Fine Arts Complex. He dropped his umbrella; she grabbed it gleefully.

"I'm so sorry—"

"Do I get to keep this?"

She wore a beige dress of obscure origin (nightgown? dress? '30s? '40s?); the rain sent it clinging against her unbound breasts, breasts almost too small for a woman, but enough—

She smiled. Her teeth were shining white. He stood in the steady rain, transfixed.

She twirled his black umbrella. The rain was slacking off. "Thanks."

He brushed the rain from his eyes. "Hey, that's my umbrella—"

She pouted. "Are you sure?"

A group of students ran by and splashed water on both of them. They turned simultaneously, groaning.

"Oh, wow—" She laughed and held the umbrella over him, reaching.

"Let me; I'm taller."

They stood for a moment, hunched close. Finally, he took an unsteady breath, gathered the courage to make the suggestion. There were pearls around her neck. He gazed at them as he heard himself speak.

"Would you like some coffee?"

"Tea."

"Tea, then."

"With you?" Her face was upturned toward him. The rain had stopped. Tendrils of hair curled about her forehead.

He cocked his head. "Yeah, who else?"

"But what's your name?" Her lips were salmon pink and curving, sweet.

"Byron."

"Lord Byron?"

"What's your name?" He ignored that remark most women had to make whenever around him. So many women, beautiful women. And this new one, so fine.

"My name is Mariana."

"Marry-anna? Well, come on, Marianna, let's go."

He closed the umbrella. She slipped her arm in his and they walked on.

He needs to sleep. He shuts his eyes too tightly; they pop open. The ceiling's blank. He punches his pillow restlessly and then checks the clock on the night table. Not enough time has ticked by. He sweats. He switches the lamp on and looks at the phone. On a repulsive impulse, he dials her number. He waits breathlessly. But no one answers. She *is* dead.

Byron decides to take a cold shower, then a hot one, then a cool one, then a warm one. At dawn he falls into a light sleep.

The next morning he combs the newspaper for an account of her death and finds nothing. He drinks black coffee and munches a piece of charred toast. He dresses for his Improvisation Class mechanically and gets there on time.

The students wait on bleachers centered around a circular stage. A few stragglers pass him. Byron watches them casually, his hands thrust in his vest pockets. A few of the girls smile at him. They always like him, the girl students. He's slept with some, discreetly, of course. He's a careful man. Sometimes.

"Situation: a man wants to kill his girlfriend; the girlfriend's trying to stay alive. Any takers?"

Hands shoot up. He picks Evans and Trowbridge. They run to the stage and throw themselves into the act. Byron tingles with the audacity of it and follows the actions of the two eagerly.

Helen Trowbridge, a short girl with curly black hair, is doing a great job but Farley Evans isn't. Byron tells him to sit down. He approaches Trowbridge himself.

"Come over here; sit down. Why are you looking at me like that?"

"I think it's time you left."

"No."

"Put that knife down—John—"

"Why don't you call me Johnny anymore?" He lifts the invisible knife to the light. It shines in his eyes. Trowbridge sees it clearly. Her acting is professional. For a moment Byron the teacher slips out, reveling in his student. He gives her a smile and then wipes it away, not wanting to throw her off track.

"You're not Johnny anymore. I don't know you. Step back; don't come any closer, please."

"You're supposed to do anything I want you to." He forces her to the floor.

She pushes him back, screaming. Then they are both silent, staring at each other.

The students wait a few seconds, then applaud. They wait for the teacher to say, "Who's next," and he struggles to his feet to follow through on their expectations. He nods at Trowbridge to indicate she's done well, and faces the others.

"Who's next?" he says weakly. For a moment no one does anything; they just look at him and he wonders if any of them know. But that's silly. The hands now go up as usual.

He stands outside "Vintage Rags, Inc.," after lunch the next day, trying to decide whether he has the courage to go in. It's where she used to work, doing alterations and manning the cashier when the owner, Kathy Ragsdale, wasn't there. He knows it's stupid but he's been thinking about the shop all morning. He can still see Mariana wearing a wide-brimmed hat, holding aloft a pearl-tipped hat pin—

"You came! Well, what do you think about the place?" She twirled her muslin petticoat and tapped the old leather boots from the early 1900s. "Aren't these wonderful? I'm the only one that can wear them. But I don't wear them very long at one time because they hurt my feet."

She put the pin in neatly and walked away from the counter. "Business is slow, Lord Byron, and I have all the time for you. Want a tour?" She grabbed his hand. Her own was edged in lace.

"This blouse is circa 1920, thereabouts. I wish Kathy was here. You'll meet her next trip, I guess. You're so quiet, Lord—what's the matter?"

"Nothing."

"Don't you like the shop?"

"Sure."

"You brought your camera. Do you want to take some shots of me in this getup? I do love it. This hat's grand." She released his hand and ran to the window by the large oaken wardrobe. "Natural light. I'll stand like this—" She held her hands to her hat and smiled.

He took his camera automatically and peered through the viewfinder. He shivered. Always like that—she commanding him, he obeying. He didn't like that. He was the man. She was supposed to be just a woman. But that face. It wasn't smiling now; it was turned profile against the light, chin down, wistful. He clicked and put the camera down.

"What's the matter, Mariana?"

She shrugged. "Nothing." She took the hat off and hung it on a nearby hat tree. She carried the hat pin to the jewelry counter and went to the chair behind the cash register. She took off the boots and slipped on her own sandals.

He stood before her expectantly.

Mariana smiled at him sadly. "I don't see much of you, and when I do see you, you are always pointing that camera at me. Does it make you see better? No, it's my fault, I guess. And if it makes you happy—" She stretched and looked toward the door. "It's really slow today." She glanced at him curiously. "It's an obsession, you know. Unless—are you serious about it—I mean, like a career?"

"No."

She blushed. "What are you going to do with all those photographs? May I have some to send to my mother and to Harriet—I told you about her. She's my best friend in New York. I grew up there."

"And I grew up in New Jersey."

"How did we ever end up in California?"

"Where flowers with bowers bloom in the sun/Each morning at dawning birdies sing and everything—" he said in singsong.

"Byron—you're crazy. Are you coming over tonight?"

"If you want me to."

"I'll make an omelette or a quiche."

They wouldn't eat much. They would make love till both were exhausted. And he might take out the camera and do nude studies while she slept.

"I love Harriet, you know," Mariana said suddenly, breaking in on his reflections.

He pictured two twelve-year-old girls holding hands adoringly —David Hamilton girls—one fair, one dark, seductively innocent.

"You love me?"

The door rang merrily as some noisy customers came in. Mariana turned to them, arms welcoming, dismissing Byron with a shake of her gentle head.

"Byron! I'm so glad to see you! Have you heard from Mariana?"

Byron feigns surprise. "What do you mean—she's not here?"

"Why no, no one can get hold of her, and Harriet's here from Brooklyn and we're just frantic."

"Did you try her house?"

"It's locked up." A black-haired woman turns from the shadows by the rack of used suits. "The window was open by the bedroom. I looked in but couldn't see much for the curtains."

His heart thunders. Rivers flow from his palms. He swallows over and over. "You're Harriet?"

"And you're Byron. Oh God, what are we going to do? Where could she be? Think we should break into the house? Call the police?"

"We could do that," he says slowly.

Kathy Ragsdale wrinkles into a confused frown. "Sit down, Byron. Harriet, he was just crazy about her. He's upset."

Harriet nods, folds her arms across her chest. She reminds Byron of a handsome Indian, implacable, calm, but filled with mute sorrow. She glances at Kathy. "And what do you think about the For Rent sign?"

Byron clenches the arms of the chair. What For Rent sign?

"Could she have moved? I couldn't see much through the windows. She didn't have much stuff, I know that, but move, without telling me, her mother—or Byron?"

"Or me, her employer," sighs Kathy.

"We really should call the police."

"I think I'm sick and need to go home for a while," mutters Byron.

"I'll call if anything develops," Kathy says.

"You call us Byron if you hear from her," Harriet says, her black eyes like ebony.

Byron stumbles from the shop, nauseated.

The last roll of film. Byron's spread out on the kitchen floor with a knife. He stabs each photograph lightly, puncturing holes where his face is in each shot. They were painful things, these, taken during an argument. Why he had taken them he couldn't fathom, but he recalls clicking away while she yelled.

"I'm so tired of this!"

Click, click.

"You don't love me; you love my picture."

Click, click.

"Byron! Stop this!"

Click, click.

"It's over with us. Do you hear me? I hate you! I hate you—God how I hate you!"

Click, click.

"You won't let me live with you. You won't marry me. And your other women—you drop your damn pants for any damn female in sight."

Click, click.

"You don't love anyone but yourself!"

They struggled, fought, ended up in a tangle of skin, Mariana begging him to say he loved her. He never did. It was like being sick. She was a disease. He gathers the ruined photos into a pile. More evidence? Three or four days have gone by. When will someone come and arrest him. He ought to be arrested.

There really is a For Rent sign in front of the little house she lived in. He saunters up the cement walk, kicks at a pebble, and crosses over into the grass. He finds himself standing before the bedroom window. He squeezes through a space in the bushes and peers inside. He smells the air. Nothing. No smells at all. He is horrified.

Someone touches his shoulder. He stiffens.

"No evidence of foul play. She's just gone."

Harriet.

"Can you believe it?" Byron says, scratching his brown mustache.

"I don't know. I haven't seen her in so long. She was behind in rent—the landlord couldn't wait. He's a real bastard. I reported her missing, but since she's an adult and it looks pretty obvious she just left—well, God knows when we'll ever hear from her again."

They step out of the bushes into the overgrown grass.

"Byron, did you two have a quarrel? Honest, did you?"

"We weren't getting along very well."

"That's it, then." She walks to her rented car, Byron tailing her with a woebegone expression. She opens the door. "Need a lift?"

"No, my car's down the street."

Her left eyebrow arches. "Well, have to meet my plane. Her mother's naturally upset. I'm thinking maybe she'll turn up on her doorstep. I hope so. I feel so bad about this. Mariana—is—well—Mariana. She's so unexpected, so headstrong in her way."

He wonders what that means. "Well, keep in touch. Here's my card."

"I left my address with Kathy if you ever need it." She smiles. Her teeth are even, perfect, white, like Mariana's were.

She starts the motor. He steps back onto the curb.

"Good-bye, Lord Byron."

"So long." The wind tosses his ragged brown hair. He thinks of them touching—Harriet and Mariana—in secret places, laughing. They probably used to bathe together, played dolls, climbed trees. He knows. Jealousy rages through him, an oily fire. It's good she's gone. It's bad, too. His throat constricts. It is not love.

He must have moved her from the bedroom but he can't remember doing it. She was definitely dead, her head hanging off the bed at an odd angle, her mouth open. How strange he can't remember burying her. Surely he should. He'll give it time.

The cat's gone. He feels lonely without Roosevelt, decides to eat without him. He eats tuna out of a can, saving a bite for the cat's bowl. He drinks white wine out of the bottle and starts to feel tight. He goes to bed early, leaving his underwear on, slobbering on his pillow like a two-year-old. He's so tired and confused. He sobs and twists the sheets around his body, wishing he'd never met her. It's not fair. He needs to be free and can't be, can't ever be. The night absorbs him. He sleeps.

Something slams into his face, waking him violently. Someone holds the other pillow down hard on his face. He pushes frantically. Mariana! He will see her again. His heart beats rapidly. Great fountains of emotion spurt upward. He manages to push a corner aside. He gazes upward in rapture for one last glimpse of her face and sees—his own.

It has been noted (and probably too often) that children have a better grasp of reality than do adults. Children know this is true about other children; adults, unfortunately, tend to be more than a little condescending when they're told that someone considerably younger knows more about what's going on out there than they do. It's a shame, because turning a deaf ear sometimes puts you directly in the path of a not-so-condescending killer.

Al Sarrantonio, once an editor, is now a full-time writer and househusband in the Bronx. He lives in a short stretch of houses flanked by apartment buildings, with enough material on his block for a dozen or more of the below.

THE MAN WITH LEGS

by Al Sarrantonio

"I don't believe you."

"You must."

"I don't."

"You will."

The proof, Nellie said, was a bus trip away.

"I have the fare," said Willie, his eyes brightening, "and I'll pay our way, and I don't believe you, and I'll make you say he isn't there."

"He is."

"Prove it."

"Only one way."

"One way," Willie sang. "One way," he said again, rolling the words over his tongue, around his lips, breathing them moist into the air.

Nellie's eyes were shadowed against his younger ones.

"I'll prove it," she said, unsmiling.

"You will," Willie echoed.

After Willie went to the bathroom (he *always* had to go to the bathroom) they set off surreptitiously. Mounting thick winter coats and mufflers, thick steamy mittens and black shiny boots, they sneaked from the house by the back door. Mother would be in the front, in the warm light of the television, watching her soap operas.

"We have two hours," Willie said, in a tone that hinted it made no difference how much time they had, their quest was so foolish.

"Plenty of time," Nellie answered.

The Saturday bus was late. They waited at the second stop from the house so Mother or one of her friends couldn't see them. Willie fingered the piggy bank in his pocket, turning open the tab that would release the money within, then turning it closed again. He stamped his feet in the cold. Nellie stood rigid, her shiny blue ski parka giving her the proportions of a snowman. Her eyes were squeezed to a squint by the hood, which she had tied tight around her face, and she avoided Willie's eyes.

"He's not there," Willie said in a slow, irritating voice.

"He *is*," Nellie replied through clenched teeth.

"It was only a dream."

"I saw him when we went by in the school bus yesterday," Nellie replied sharply. "I saw him as plain as the lips on your mouth. He was standing on the porch of his house, and he looked at me as the bus went by."

"You dreamed it."

"Didn't."

"You'll never find the house."

"I marked it in my mind."

" 'Nuff said."

She turned to hit him, but her bulky swing made her miss. That only made Willie grin.

"Does. Not. Exist," he said, waving his hands at her in a taunting way.

She scooped up snow and heaved it awkwardly at him.

"You'll see plenty."

They stood silent in the snow, waiting for the bus, slapping at their bodies. The temperature had dipped. The light was bright off the crusted snow; if they hadn't liked snow so much it would have hurt their eyes.

"I don't believe you," Willie said.

At that moment the bus came.

They climbed on huffing, and Willie broke open his bank, spilling the change into his palm. They had just enough. He held back a quarter a moment, scaring Nellie into thinking there wasn't enough, and then dropped it into the receptacle, smiling at the driver. The driver didn't smile back. They moved to the middle of the bus, choosing two seats on what Nellie said was the "right" side.

"Why not the other side? We're not going to see the house anyway."

"Sit," Nellie said.

The bus was warm. They contented themselves by watching the patterns of snow outside. There were snow valleys and peaks and stiff, hard drifts of white that sloped up the sides of buildings and stayed there. Willie watched the passing houses, dreamlike in their frosting; he enjoyed especially the upside-down ice-cream-cone icicles that hung frozen from all corners, some dipping to just touch the drifts below.

"Brrr," Nellie said, looking at the same scene and at the ring of frost around the bus window itself.

"It's beautiful," Willie sighed, turning to frown at her.

"Brrr," she said again, challenging him. "You're just too young to know how cold it is."

He shrugged and turned back, admiring the rainbow sheen of ice on a line of row houses. In his mind, all the world became a snowball, an ice shell four inches deep made of snowmen and newspaper delivery boys in parkas and ski boots.

"There it is," Nellie said suddenly, giving him a hard shove. "That's it."

Willie looked along her finger, out past the tip, through the ice-free hole in the window to the spot she indicated.

"I still don't believe you," he said, but his voice was a whisper and he knew he was lying.

There lay a house different from the others, set alone on a small lot with space on either side. Though surrounded by row houses, it stood squarely out. It looked like a boarding house, blocklike and looming, its windows making a face and its porch, stretching from end to end, making a mouth. The house stood off the ground on stilts and, in the snow, looked like a brooding, sly white spider.

"I'll make you believe me," Nellie said. She was already reaching for the pull-cord to let them off the bus when Willie's hand reached for hers. He wanted to stop her. He wanted to stay on the warm bus and look at the frosty world outside and then take it around the circle of its route back to his own house and get off. Then he wanted to make a quick snow fort and get inside in time for supper.

"I believe you, let's go home," he said.

Nellie stood, smiling a smirk down at him.

"I told you it was real."

"You're older than me," Willie said in answer.

"I know," she said, pulling the cord and beginning to walk up the aisle as the bus pulled to a puffing halt at the curb.

He pulled on his mitten, which he had taken off to empty his bank and which had swung loose on its tie to his snowsuit cuff, and ran after her as her head bobbed out of sight down the steps of the exit.

They stood alone at the corner as the bus coughed away.

The afternoon was deathly still. Even the noise of a car with clanking chains on its wheels would have disturbed the Universe at this moment, and both of them knew in their hearts that no such car would come by. Even the frozen telephone wires stood still, the breeze that had whistled them all day quieting in respect.

"Let's go," Nellie said, stepping into the street. Her foot made an agreeable crunch.

Willie stepped hesitantly after her.

They crossed the street hand in hand, and only then, when they stood on the opposite curb in front of the white spider house, did the world begin to turn again.

A car with chains on its wheels churned by.

"I told you I believe you," Willie said, trying to put his hand back into hers.

She wouldn't take it.

"But I don't know if I believe myself," she said tentatively.

They crunched up the porch steps, which creaked woodenly, even under their coating of ice. Someone had salted the steps liberally, and their boots gripped so well on them that Willie imagined that hands had grown up out of the wood and were pulling his boots up, plank by plank.

When they reached the top step Nellie pointed.

"That was where I saw him," she said, "right in front of that window next to the door."

"I . . . don't know," Willie said.

She reached for the bell, and this time his hand found hers first and held it tight.

"Please."

She turned her eyes on him, and her eyes said, Tell me the reason, the only reason, why I should stop.

"Because I don't want to know," Willie said in a small sob.

"You do want to know," she said evenly. "And I have to."

Her hand slipped through his and hit the bell solidly.

Somewhere deep within the house a deep, deep chime sounded.

Dong. Dong.

Silence.

Nellie hit the bell again, longer this time, keeping her mitten on it.

Dong. Dong. Dong. Dong.

Deep within, footsteps.

Hesitating at first, the steps of someone unsure, and then firmer and more resolute.

They took a long time to reach the door, but Nellie and Willie waited.

Dong. Dong.

Nellie pulled her hand away from the bell.

The door, a narrow tooth in the house-spider's mouth, opened. Someone stared out at them and said, "Yes?"

Nellie stumbled back, her eyes wide.

"Fa-" she began, faltering.

"-ther," Willie finished, his mouth hanging open.

Before them stood a young man with black tousled hair and a boyish expression on his open face. His mouth was half-smiling, ready for anything. There was a faint tobacco smell about him and about his flannel shirt. He wore suspenders.

"Pardon me?" he said, a look of bemusement crossing his features.

"I, you—" Willie began.

"Father," Nellie stated simply.

The man's eyebrows went up, but the smile did not leave his lips.

"What she means is, we *thought* you were our father," Willie said. He took his sister's hand, started to pull her back down the porch steps.

Nellie's feet resisted in the snow.

"No," she said. "I was right." She turned back to the man in the doorway. "You're our father."

"Oh? Can that be possible?" The man was staring down past their faces, at their rubber boots.

"Can it?" Nellie said, faltering. She stood with her hands at her side, suddenly becoming conscious that they were hands and that she must do something with them. She put them into her pockets.

"Mother told us you died," Willie blurted out.

The man considered for a moment, then opened the door wider.

"Come in out of the cold," he said.

Nellie began to tramp her feet on the mat, but Willie held back.

"I really didn't think it could be you," Willie said, mostly to himself.

"Come in," the man said softly.

There was the sound of him closing the door behind them with a chilly whoosh, and then the warmth of the house began to seep in. It was almost too warm.

"Into the living room," he said, moving in front of them.

It was now that Willie saw his limp. He moved stiffly, like a man on stilts, and though the expression on his face didn't seem to change, Willie could sense an effort behind it, a grunt held back at each step.

"Sit down," the man offered. They settled into a huge green sofa that gobbled them up halfway in oversoft cushions. "Take your coats off." The man sat on a stiff-back chair, pulling it up opposite them across the polished floor. He lowered himself onto it with strain. A fire, a large fire, burned off to their right, and the room was dark but for its amber light and the hint of blue snow-illumination that seeped in from the wide window by the front door.

Neither moved to take off their coats.

"We have to get back on the bus soon," Nellie explained. She wouldn't take her eyes off him. "She told us you died."

"Did she," the man said, meeting her eyes and holding them. "That's interesting." The smile softened around his mouth, making him look even more like a boy.

"Were you hurt in a train wreck?" Willie said tactlessly. "Is that why you limp?"

The man's eyes darted to the floor before rising to meet his.

"No," he said simply. His eyes lingered on Willie's legs before moving back to Nellie.

"He was too young to remember when it happened," she explained. "But I remember. They all said you were killed when the train you were on missed a signal and hit the back of another train. They . . . said your legs had been cut off."

"Is that what they said?"

"Yes."

"I suppose they were wrong then."

"Father," Nellie breathed, trying the word on.

The man nodded slowly in answer.

"How long have you been hiding?" said Willie. He was beginning to grow uncomfortable on the couch, and unzipped his parka halfway. He still looked sullen.

"We can't stay long," Nellie scolded, "at least not this time."

The man smiled.

"How long hiding?" Willie insisted.

The man drew his breath in and considered. "Let me see," he said. "It must be . . ." He counted on his fingers. "Five years."

As he said this his fingers tapped lightly on his legs.

"Why?" Nellie asked. "Why did you have to hide?"

"I had to go away." He suddenly slapped his knees, making as if to get up. "Why don't I get us some hot chocolate at least? You must still be cold. We can talk more then."

"We really have to go soon."

"Please?" The pleading in his voice was startling, it came so sudden.

"All right," Nellie said quickly. "We . . . really don't know you very well."

"That's true."

He got up with a nonfluid motion, gasping as he stood finally on his feet, using the back of his chair for support.

"Are you all right?" Nellie asked.

"Yes," he said. His eyes seemed glued to her foot and then he hoisted himself erect, like a straw man. "I'll be back in a moment."

He disappeared into the rear of the house.

"Do you believe me now?" Nellie said.

"He does look like the picture in Mother's bedroom," Willie admitted sulkily. "But I don't like him."

"I *do.*" She overemphasized this last word. "He just hasn't seen us in a long time."

Willie rose. "I don't like the way he walks. Like a stiff man."

"Where are you going?"

"Bathroom," Willie stated.

"Wait till he comes back."

"If he's really Father, I can go to the bathroom."

"He has to be."

Willie moved off, shaking his head.

He quickly became lost. Going through the door the man had gone through, he found himself in a mazelike corridor unlike the rest of the house. Cracked green and white tiles covered the floor, and the walls were peeling with paint. One corridor led off to another, and another, and soon Willie found himself surrounded by branching passageways in an ever-increasing darkness; dim fireflylike bulbs overhead gave illumination.

Willie moved slowly, fingering the walls, until a sound down one corridor pulled him toward it.

A high, singing sound and, behind that, the sound of metal against metal.

Willie stopped before a door, eased it open a crack and peered in.

There were steps leading down, faintly lit, and an area below with more light spread around it.

Down there, someone was singing.

A happy voice—but like the sound a cat makes when you step on its tail accidentally.

The clashing metal stopped.

The singing stopped.

There was a grunt and the sound of something being lashed and tied, the whipping of ropes, and then footsteps.

Little, dancing footsteps, more grunting, and then steadier steps.

Someone was on the stairs.

Willie arched back around the doorway, leaning into the darkness.

After a long, long time, in which Willie counted twenty slow steps, the door was eased open in front of his face. It was closed, and Willie found himself staring at the back of the man who was Father. The man's flannel shirt was hiked up, and Willie could see a network of fine straps crisscrossing his back, pulled tight.

The man moved off toward the front of the house.

Willie counted to fifty and then emerged from the shadows. Holding his breath, he edged open the cellar door and peered down. The light was still on. He edged himself down two steps and crouched, cocking his head. There were no sounds in the cellar.

He went all the way down.

Gasped.

Though he knew she wasn't there, he called out involuntarily, "Oh, Nellie."

On the walls of the room, on every wall in the room, hanging on pegs, in rows, sticking out from boxes, piled in corners, were—

Legs.

There were hundreds, maybe thousands of pairs of legs. In all lengths and sizes, they were squatty and wrist-thin and beefy and babylike. Each was dressed appropriately, in pants or stockings, socks and shoes, ballerina slippers, bedroom slippers, Italian leather shoes or cordovan penny-loafers. Willie could almost see the rest of the people they should be attached to: bankers and bakers and newspaper delivery boys; shoe salesmen; funeral directors. There was a pair with big brown thick boots that looked like they belonged to the man who cleans sewers. There were two or three tap dancers. A gas station attendant. A janitor. All had straps at the top and fine webbings and clasps and snaps and thongs.

There was just about one pair of legs for anything you could imagine.

"Oh, Nellie," Willie breathed, wanting his sister to be there, to hold his hand.

The only other thing in the room besides legs was a small table in the far corner, laid out neatly under a low neon lamp which caught the clean white light off its racks of toothy blades, perfectly outlining them.

Saws. Racks and racks of long and sinewy saws, special bright silver ones that liked to do their work.

"Oh Nellie, Nellie," Willie whispered.

From above, a sound sounded.

A light step on the stair.

A sneaky step.

Holding his breath, Willie turned.

A face peeked under the stair at him, upside down.

"Nellie!"

"Shhh!"

She disappeared back up the stair. Willie heard the click of the closing door, and then she was down in front of him.

Willie began to pull her toward the walls of legs. "Nellie, he—"

"He told me," she said, hushing him. "He told me everything."

"Where is he?" Willie gasped.

"Upstairs." Her eyes got a sly look. "I told him the bus driver was Mother's boyfriend and that he'd be coming for us now unless someone waved him on."

"What are we going to do?" Willie said fearfully.

"He wants us to stay," Nellie said simply.

"No!"

"He's not bad, Willie. Most of his legs he dug up, or found on people who were already dead."

"But—"

"If we stay, he says he'll be Father most of the time. I want him to be Father."

"But Nellie—"

"I *need* that, Willie. Just like he needs to be the people whose legs he puts on."

"I want to go home! I don't want him!"

Trembling, Willie grabbed his sister round the waist and hugged her.

On her back, beneath her hiked-up ski parka and blouse, Willie felt clasps and buckles and straps.

"You!" he cried, pushing her away.

"Yes," Nellie said icily. Willie saw now how stiffly she moved.

"Nellie!" Willie sobbed.

"I can be anything in this room," Nellie said, turning stiffly and stabbing her finger at the walls and boxes. "I can be the man who delivers flowers, the woman who gives piano lessons. I can be the mailman one morning, the insurance man who comes to your house the same night. Your teacher. Priest. Dentist." She loped toward the neon-lit workbench and lifted with a click from its rack a crystal-fine saw.

"I can be," Nellie said, rocking rigidly on her legs and tossing her diamond sawblade into the air, catching it nimbly, "a little girl. Or little boy."

Willie leaped for the stairs, landing painfully on his knees on the second step from the bottom. Scrambling up them on all fours, he hit the closed door at the top.

It wouldn't open.

Nellie came slowly up after him. There was a smile on her face that the real Nellie had never worn—an ancient smile, nothing even like the meanest smile she had put on when doing the meanest big-sister thing to him.

When she was two steps from him, Willie kicked out at her legs.

"Nooo!" she cried out, falling backward.

Dreamlike, Nellie's body split in two. The bottom half, two leaden appendages trailing snapped strings and wires at the top, clacked dully down the steps to land dead at the bottom.

The top half changed into something else. No longer Nellie, no longer anything human—mailman, priest, or dentist—it turned into a screaming white thing, a shriveled form that scooted down the stairs like an albino insect on two deformed hands.

"Noooooo!" it cooed, moving past the two legs at the bottom of the stair toward the back of the room.

Willie pushed desperately against the cellar door, and with a sudden jerk it opened. Once again he found himself in a maze. Green and white tiled floors assaulted his feet, trying to make him trip. He made turn after turn and found himself back in front of the cellar door. From below he heard a high keening scream that made his bones rattle. He stumbled on, pushing at the walls, trying to find a way out.

Abruptly, Willie found himself in the living room. The same hot fire roared in the fireplace, the same overstuffed olive furniture squatted in front of it.

He ran past, out to the front door. There it was, and next to it the wide window to the outside world. Where snow forts waited, and television, and dinner, and Mother.

Miraculously, as he looked, the bus chugged to a halt at the stop outside the house, waiting.

His hand was on the doorknob.

Pulling it open.

A foot stepped around him to press the door closed.

And a voice, the puffing voice of someone who had run very fast very quietly, the voice of someone he might have known, said, "Walk with me, won't you?"

Monsters of all sorts stalk the nightmares of pregnant women and fathers-to-be. It's inevitable when the news media are constantly warning us that this favorite food and that favorite drink have suddenly been discovered to cause wretched diseases in laboratory animals. The problem with nightmares like this, however, is that they don't always end when the sun comes up . . . and they don't always end at all.

Leigh Kennedy's work has appeared in Terry Carr's Universe *as well as other periodicals and anthologies, and she is as gentle in person as this story is not.*

THE SILENT CRADLE

by Leigh Kennedy

Florie O'Bannon first suspected that she had a third child about mid-October.

The room at the end of the hall had been relegated to storage, mostly furnishings that Vanessa and Tim had grown out of. Florie opened the door, expecting disarray. The old crib that both children had used stood against one wall, a yellow blanket draped across the rail, as if to keep the bright sun off the mattress.

There was the smell of soured milk.

Florie stood for a moment, rubbing her arms. Everything had been packed away into the closet except those things an infant would need. A clean, dry bottle stood on the bedside stand, which was filled with folded diapers.

She walked to the window, trying to remember when she had last come into this room. A month . . . two months? She remembered closing the door one evening in late summer to hide the clutter from company. She opened the window to air out the strange smell.

"Now, why did I come in here?" she asked aloud. She'd completely forgotten. Coming through the window, the breeze was cool. Too cool. Instinctively, she shut the window.

She walked back to the living room, filled with a nostalgia about newborns. Vanessa was now eight; Tim five. Both had been joys to her at all ages, and yet sometimes she thought the newborn's day most magical, like the first days of a love affair. She had only wanted to stare at their wrinkled faces and fondle their toes.

She sat down cross-legged in front of the bookcase where they kept the baby albums.

There was a new one. Like the others, it had a padded white binding. Tentatively, Florie pulled it out and opened it.

Born: October 11, 7:45 A.M., 8 lbs., 4 oz., 21½ inches. George Russell O'Bannon.

No picture.

Florie reread the entry absently, trying to imagine what sort of joke her husband might be playing on her. He'd often told her that she enjoyed children more than discretion allowed, that two would certainly be enough. No, this was not the kind of thing he would do. The smell of milk, the casualness of the blanket on the crib . . . These things were apart from his senses, too subtle for his kind of joke.

Florie closed the book and put it away. Momentarily, she felt guilty. Yes, she would love to have another child, and for a moment she could pretend. When Tim came storming in from the backyard, calling, "Mom! Mom!" she thought that she might shush him. The baby was sleeping.

But she said nothing. She would wait to see who would finally break down and laugh with her about the book and the room.

Florie paused in the hallway. Vanessa stood at the crib with her face wedged between the side rails. An empty bottle lay in the crib.

"What are you doing?" Florie asked.

Vanessa looked up, embarrassed. "Just looking," Vanessa said.

"At what?" Florie realized that she sounded sterner than necessary out of a sudden flutter of nerves.

"Just looking," Vanessa said.

Children have a way of looking obviously secretive without knowing the adult ability to follow such nuances. Florie smiled at her daughter's coyness, feeling a flush of recognition for her as an individual. "Did you put the bottle in there?" Florie saw a thin white residue on one side.

"No." Vanessa pulled away from the crib and started past Florie without looking up.

"What are you thinking about, little one?" Florie asked, brushing her hand over Vanessa's silky hair.

"Ms. Harley asked me how my new little brother was," she said in a tone of confession.

Florie knelt and looked Vanessa in the eye. "We don't have a baby," she said. "Did you come in here to look?"

Vanessa nodded. "I thought maybe he was a secret."

Florie laughed. "It would be hard to keep that a secret, wouldn't it? Besides, wouldn't I want you to help me with a new baby?"

Vanessa smiled briefly, then a question appeared in her eyes again. "But what was that sound I heard the other night?"

"What sound?" Florie was chilled.

"It sounded like a baby crying."

Florie paused to pull herself together. "It may have been some cats in the yard."

Vanessa gave her a doubtful look but said nothing. After Vanessa went to the kitchen, Florie looked back at the silent crib. She pulled the door to.

Quietly.

The meat loaf is too salty, she thought, shaking the ketchup bottle over her plate.

"I can't imagine how a rumor like this got started, Florie," her husband said. "Don't they remember the picnic this summer? You were in shorts and a halter top. Don't they remember Bridget's birthday party? That was only a few months ago."

"Don't know, Bert," she said.

The children looked from their plates to the parents, fork tines down in their mouths, eyes curious. Tim had a milk mustache.

Florie had hoped her husband could clear up the whole affair. But in the last few minutes he had proved to be as puzzled as herself. "Well, whoever it is, is close to us," she said. And she rose to fetch the baby book she'd found.

There were new entries: a month-old birth weight and a note of the six-weeks checkup. "Healthy!" it said. She found an envelope stuck between the pages. Her husband took the book and leafed through it, frowning. "What *is* this?" he said.

She laughed. And then she began to giggle, self-consciously, knowing her amusement wasn't shared yet. Tears wet her lashes.

"Florie?" Bert said. "What's going on? Are you trying to tell me something?"

She handed him the paper and envelope which she'd just read. "He's a cheap kid anyway."

Bert smiled vaguely as he read the receipt from the pediatrician. Paid. They both ignored Vanessa's persistent, "What? What is it?"

"Florie, it's a funny joke," Bert said flatly.

"But it's not mine," she said, smiling.

Tim looked back and forth between his parents with reserve. "Mom, can I have more potatoes?"

At Christmas, Florie put a teddy bear under the tree tagged "Russell." Vanessa wanted it, but Florie playfully viewed it as a sacrifice to the prank. Into the crib it went.

By Easter it was worn. Florie thought that the children played with it surreptitiously.

By summer there had been other notes and receipts in the baby book. Florie discovered that Russell cut his first tooth earlier than her other children.

By fall she found pieces of zwieback on the floor. Anything at the edge of counters was likely to be pulled off.

She said little about it to Bert. In the beginning they had figured it lightly. But now, guiltily, she took pleasure in the situation. She no longer thought about who was pulling the prank or why.

Now that Tim was in school whole days, she'd begun to go shopping, visiting with her mother and a few nonworking friends.

She would pause at the door, staring inward, uneasy about leaving.

Whenever she stood in the extra room she felt a kind of warm spookiness. As if someone were thinking of her strongly and lovingly. She set up her sewing machine in the room. Then a comfortable chair for reading by the window.

More and more often she found an excuse to spend time by the crib.

"Florie," Bert called.

She thought he was in their bedroom, but she found him in the spare room. He was holding a small wooden truck. Bert looked stern, as he did when he had to do or say something he didn't relish.

"What's the matter?" she asked.

"We can't afford for you to be buying things like this for foolishness."

"What!" She looked at the truck. Like the mobile that hung over the crib—little blue ducks and yellow fish swimming midair —like the rattlers and teething rings, it had just suddenly been there. Where it had come from, she had no idea.

"Listen, Florie," Bert said patiently. "I know you would like to have another baby."

"Wait a minute," she said. "I don't have anything to do with this."

Bert sighed. "Why can't you just talk to me about it anymore? What's happened to you?"

Florie shook her head. "You've got it all wrong. I haven't done any of this. Well, I bought the teddy," she said, picking it up out of the crib. She felt a pang, wondering if somehow she really was responsible for whatever was going on. But how? She knew in her mind that soon a friend, her mother, or even Vanessa would own up to it.

"We can't afford this joke anymore," Bert said.

Florie knew that things were tight. Their car had thrown a rod a few months ago and they'd unexpectedly been forced to buy a new one. They'd had to have the plumber out a few times. School clothes were expensive this year, and Christmas was on the way. Prices were going up.

"Bert, believe me," Florie said.

He studied her for a long while. "I don't know what to say. I think we need for you to go back to work, even just half days."

"Bert . . ."

He put his arms around her, teddy and all. "I think it will be good for you. I suspect you're bored."

Stunned, Florie said nothing. Perhaps he was right.

She sat at her desk and squirmed. As if she itched, she longed to scratch, but she couldn't localize it. She simply was uncomfortable.

She pleaded illness and rushed home. In the bathroom a tub of cloudy tepid water stood, and a box of baking soda sat on the floor. Florie looked in the spare room. It was hot and stuffy, but she didn't dare open the window.

She lay on her bed, feeling safely at home, but worried. Worried about what, she didn't know. By now she was used to finding unexplained things. She dozed.

As she slept, she seemed to be aware of her sleeping self— knowing where she was and why. And in that awareness she held close to her the shape of a toddler wrapped in a blanket. The child was restless, his fever radiated through the blanket to her.

"It's all right, Russell," she said in her sleep. She comforted him just as she had Vanessa and Tim, thanking God that she had already had chicken pox.

She was furious the day she came home and the kitchen was ravaged. Pots and pans, dishes and tin cans had been pulled out of the cupboards. A stick of butter hadn't yet melted enough to hide the teethmarks.

She yelled at Russell from the living room, to be sure that he heard her from wherever he was. But he was too young to understand yet, for the situation didn't improve until the receipts from the day-care center began arriving.

"Mom," Tim said, "Russell broke the crib."

Florie looked at Bert.

Bert stood. "Now, look, young man. That's going too far. You can't blame things on an imaginary being. What did you do?"

"I didn't do it," Tim said with the certainty of a clear conscience. "I heard a noise a while ago and now the crib's busted. Come and look."

Florie saw that Bert believed Tim's honesty but not the story. They followed him into Russell's room. The slats of the crib had been smashed outward.

"The bed's too small for him now," she said calmly.

"That's stupid," Bert said. "I think . . ." He shrugged. "This whole thing is stupid." And he stalked away.

They bought Timothy a new bed, had the crib hauled away, and sent Tim's old bed into the extra room. Florie went to a secondhand store and bought a bedspread for the old bed. She cleaned out the baby things and had a garage sale. All of Tim's old clothes went into Russell's dresser.

Sometimes she found them in the laundry hamper.

Tim spent time playing in Russell's room. Bert noticed it, explaining that Tim probably missed his old bed. (He never did see the need for the new one.) "Besides," he said, "we don't yell at him when he bounces on it anymore."

Vanessa found blood on the back porch one day. A few days later, a receipt came for nine stitches at the clinic.

Bert raged. "I've had enough of this!"

He called Dr. Thorn. After explaining the four-year-old prank to the pediatrician, whom Florie had always been reluctant to discuss it with, the doctor only said, "I don't know what to tell you. According to our records, Russell has always been seen by my partner, who only works on Wednesday afternoons."

"What the *hell* is going on around here?"

"I don't know, Mr. O'Bannon. Maybe you should hold a séance."

Florie heard Bert say something she thought improper and impolite. Embarrassed, she took her children to another pediatrician the next time.

One day the kitchen window was shattered by a baseball. Vanessa and Tim were not home. Florie saw no one in the yard.

Everyone disavowed responsibility for the leftovers being set out for a persistent stray dog. Eventually the dog won his way into the family. He never answered to the name they gave him and always slept on Russell's bed. Much later he got a silver tag and they found out that his name was Claude. Claude was a quiet dog; he always seemed to be waiting and listening.

Vanessa told Florie matter-of-factly that Russell would sometimes come into her room at night and hold her hand. In fact, Vanessa seemed to be his favorite. She found unexplained treats in her room—sometimes candy, sometimes a new comic book. On her sixteenth birthday she received a record. It was Vanessa who'd started long ago having a birthday celebration every October for her youngest brother.

When Russell started school, Tim tried dutifully (at Florie's instruction) to check on Russell in class. Tim was too bashful to speak to the teachers. He peeked in the windows, but saw no one he could positively identify as his brother. So Florie tried herself. He was always either on a field trip or out of the room working on a special project.

Florie found report cards in his room, along with the baseballs, comic books, jars of grasshoppers, magnifying glasses, bits of junk picked up along the walk from school to home. He was a good student, though "Shy and hard to communicate with verbally," as his second-grade teacher put it.

He left his parents cards on the dinner table every holiday.

Russell was treated like a fact by the children. What to them had been a bit of amusement their parents had thought up turned into a person that was always not quite there yet, or had just left. Russell's doings were reported at the dinner table.

Florie had forgotten that it was a joke. When people asked her about her children, she would say, "I have three . . ." and hesitate, or she would say she had two and be just as uncertain.

Bert didn't see it their way. The evening before Russell's eighth birthday, Bert stopped Vanessa midsentence as she talked about the cake she was going to bake.

"Enough!" he shouted.

Florie, Vanessa, and Tim stared, each shaken.

"There is no Russell, there never has been a Russell, and there never will be," Bert said, leaning toward Vanessa. "You," he said to Florie, "have two children. *Two*, Florie. This one"—he pointed to Vanessa, then to Tim—"and this one. I have no son named Russell."

"Aw, Dad," Tim said, as if this were an old argument.

"Show me," Bert said, pounding his fist on the table. "Show me!"

"Vanessa, why don't you and Tim clean up the kitchen," Florie said. She stood and held out her hand to Bert. "Let's take a walk."

Bert sat at the table until Florie brought him his jacket. He put it on and walked out of the house ahead of her. They strolled silently for a time. Florie took his hand.

Bert kicked at some leaves. "You take it for granted. I just can't. Eight years, Florie. I just can't handle it anymore. It's not funny, and yet I can't take it seriously. You can't really believe all this, can you?"

Florie shrugged. "You remember what I told you about my family? When we were growing up—the door would blow open and we would say, 'It's our ghost.'" And we said our ghost took things, broke things, did this or that. It just got to be something we said. I don't know, love. Maybe it's the same one, only now he's got a name and a place."

Bert looked at her. "Well, is he real or not?"

Florie paused.

"Is he real?" Bert insisted.

"I . . . don't know."

He shrugged.

After a silence, he said, "You know, I've been thinking about something old Dr. Thorn said years ago. Something we should have done sooner."

"What's that?"

Bert laughed a little. He hesitated long enough to let Florie know that he was embarrassed. "Maybe we should have a séance."

They both laughed. Florie took his arm and felt good that they were laughing together. "Are you serious?" she asked, still giggling.

"Oh, I don't know, love. It couldn't hurt."

They heard a rustle of dried leaves in the yard they passed. Both looked, but neither saw anything. Bert frowned as he swung Florie back toward the house.

Then they laughed again as they ran.

If there could be a medium with respectability, references, and an honest, no hocus-pocus air, it was Barbara. She was young, slim, blond, and matter-of-fact. Florie had found her through a psychiatrist's reference and checked her out thoroughly.

First she listened with a pen and notepad to the whole story. She looked at Russell's room, handled some of his possessions, looked at his handwriting carefully. Florie felt odd watching those long fingers touching his things, as if that made Russell more real. Quietly, Barbara asked what kind of person they thought he was, and everyone agreed that he was a good kind of kid—no one had ever complained. He'd only done things that any boy would do. Florie chuckled about the worms in the kitchen sink (in retrospect.)

Barbara sat and explained to all of them that séances didn't often work. Rarely, in fact. But there seemed to be a strong possibility of a ghost. Why, she didn't know, unless there was a strong desire for this addition to the family that had attracted Russell.

Florie looked at her hands, guiltily avoiding Bert's face. She shivered. She realized that she'd never thought of Russell as a *ghost*, really. More a *spirit*.

"Well, do you think this is a good idea?" Barbara asked. "Suppose we do contact him?"

Florie and Bert looked at one another. Florie tried to figure her feelings about it; Bert seemed to be watching her face for the answer.

"Shall we go ahead?" Barbara asked patiently.

Florie gave Bert an "I-don't-see-why-not" look, and he nodded.

"I don't see why not," he said.

Barbara joked with Tim about his cold hands as they sat down at the dining room table. Tim's bashfulness was apparent even in the dim light. Barbara talked calmly to Russell, asking him to appear. She spoke to him as if he were shy. Then she turned to Vanessa. "You talk to him."

Vanessa stared at the table. "It won't work."

Barbara raised her eyebrows just a little. "Why?"

"Because . . ." She looked at Barbara in that quiet way that adolescent girls look at young women. "Séances are for *dead* people."

The hairs on the back of Florie's neck rose.

The family looked at Barbara for the answer. Barbara half-smiled as she considered. "Maybe you're right."

Florie glanced at Bert, who sighed. He looked worn and just a bit depressed. Barbara let go of Tim and Vanessa's hands. "Why don't we rest up. And if you decide you want to try again, we'll get together another night." She stood.

They were quiet as they watched her gather her notes almost absently. "Keep in touch," she said as she left.

Florie woke and reached out into the space beside her in the bed. She listened for a while to the early morning sounds, trying to discover the movement of her husband in the house somewhere. She slid out of the warm covers and padded through the room into the hallway. Softly, she called Bert's name.

The door to Russell's room was slightly open. Quietly, she pushed it open. Bert sat in a chair by the bed. He lifted his sleepy chin from his chest and looked at her bleary-eyed. He put his finger to his lips.

They returned to their room. "What is it?" she whispered, climbing back into bed.

"I'm not sure. I think he had a nightmare or something."

He held her as they fell asleep again. Florie felt something had changed, but Bert never talked much about it again.

When Vanessa went to college, Russell missed her so much that he apparently spent his evenings in her room reading; his books were sometimes in a neat stack by her bed. Claude took to napping on her rug, too.

Tim became interested in computers in high school and found that his brother borrowed his magazines and books on that subject. Tim said that he figured sometimes he went to Willie's with him. Willie had a micro-computer. They sometimes found funny messages on the screen. When Florie asked what kind of messages, Tim told her that Russell suggested a computer game of hide-and-seek which they worked out and had a lot of fun with.

Florie was more embarrassed when she found the men's magazines under Russell's bed than she ever had been about Tim's. (She had been sure she was alone when she found Tim's.)

Tim went off to college.

Russell liked his schoolwork; his reports were always excellent. He won an essay award while a junior in high school, which Florie found on his dresser and framed on his wall. He left his term papers out, which Florie and Bert read with amazement.

He seemed fascinated with international relations, history, and economics.

"Oh, Bert," Florie said once, "what if he goes into espionage?"

Bert assured her that he may be elusive, but he left too many clues to be a spy.

His high school yearbooks showed up on the bedroom bookshelf. Russell O'Bannon was always listed—in fact, he belonged to the computer club, Latin club, and Honor Society. He was never available for photos, however.

In the summer of his eighteenth year, the house became uncommonly lonely. Claude wagged his tail wistfully every now and then as he sniffed through Russell's room. Florie expanded her part-time job to full-time. It wasn't easy at first to enjoy the new solitude. The holidays were the same as ever; Christmas brought a full round of presents, including gifts from Russell. He'd developed a real knack for getting something for everyone that they'd never really wished for but was a marvelous gift just the same.

Bert and Florie received the paid tuition notices from a prestigious and expensive university. Russell was apparently working several part-time jobs through the school year, including gopher work at a law firm.

He attended Vanessa's wedding but didn't make it back for summer vacation of his second year.

It was that summer, his twentieth year, when the mailgram from Italy came.

"Look," Florie said, waving it at Bert. They had been receiving postcards from England, France, and Spain for the last month. Without a close look, she tore the thin envelope open.

"What is it?" Bert said.

Florie went numb. She sat down with the letter fluttering in her hand.

Bert took the letter from her.

They wept, then called Vanessa and Tim.

Russell had been killed in a terrorist explosion at a small Italian airport. The American Embassy had written, expressing terrible regret for their loss and that the students he'd been traveling with had said only wonderful things about their brilliant young son.

Florie found Bert sitting on Russell's bed. She sat down beside him and leaned her cheek against his shoulder.

She decided then that they would keep the room just as it had been when Russell was alive.

It's nice when people take a liking to you; not so nice when that liking turns them into leeches not necessarily natural. They're like shadows on an occasionally lighted street—just when you think they're gone, you look behind you . . .

David Morrell, author of First Blood, The Totem, *and* Blood Oath, *among others, is an unassuming and delightful man who teaches in Iowa, and who swears that ninety percent of the following story is true.*

BUT AT MY BACK I ALWAYS HEAR

by David Morrell

She phoned again last night. At 3 A.M. the way she always does. I'm scared to death. I can't keep running. On the hotel's register downstairs, I lied about my name, address, and occupation, hoping to hide from her. My real name's Charles Ingram. Though I'm here in Johnstown, Pennsylvania, I'm from Iowa City, Iowa. I teach—or used to teach until three days ago—creative writing at the University. I can't risk going back there. But I don't think I can hide much longer. Each night, she comes closer.

From the start, she scared me. I came to school at eight to prepare my classes. Through the side door of the English building I went up a stairwell to my third-floor office, which was isolated by a fire door from all the other offices. My colleagues used to joke that I'd been banished, but I didn't care, for in my far-off corner I could concentrate. Few students interrupted me. Regardless of the busy noises past the fire door, I sometimes felt there was no one else inside the building. And indeed at 8 A.M. I often *was* the only person in the building.

That day I was wrong, however. Clutching my heavy briefcase, I trudged up the stairwell. My scraping footsteps echoed off the walls of pale-red cinderblock, the stairs of pale-green imitation marble. First floor. Second floor. The neon lights glowed coldly. Then the stairwell angled toward the third floor, and I saw her waiting on a chair outside my office. Pausing, I frowned up at her. I felt uneasy.

Eight A.M., for you, is probably not early. You've been up for quite a while so you can get to work on time or get your children off to school. But 8 A.M., for college students, is the middle of the night. They don't like morning classes. When their schedules force them to attend one, they don't crawl from bed until they absolutely have to, and they don't come stumbling into class until I'm just about to start my lecture.

I felt startled, then, to find her waiting ninety minutes early. She sat tensely: lifeless dull brown hair, a shapeless dingy sweater, baggy faded jeans with patches on the knees and frays around the cuffs. Her eyes seemed haunted, wild, and deep and dark.

I climbed the last few steps and, puzzled, stopped before her. "Do you want an early conference?"

Instead of answering, she nodded bleakly.

"You're concerned about a grade I gave you?"

This time, though, in pain she shook her head from side to side.

Confused, I fumbled with my key and opened the office, stepping in. The room was small and narrow: a desk, two chairs, a wall of bookshelves, and a window. As I sat behind the desk, I watched her slowly come inside. She glanced around uncertainly. Distraught, she shut the door.

That made me nervous. When a female student shuts the door, I start to worry that a colleague or a student might walk up the stairs and hear a female voice and wonder what's so private I want to keep the door closed. Though I should have told her to reopen it, her frantic eyes aroused such pity in me that I sacrificed my principle, deciding her torment was so personal she could talk about it only in strict secrecy.

"Sit down." I smiled and tried to make her feel at ease, though I myself was not at ease. "What seems to be the difficulty, Miss . . . ? I'm sorry, but I don't recall your name."

"Samantha Perry. I don't like 'Samantha,' though." She fidgeted. "I've shortened it to—"

"Yes? To what?"

"To 'Sam'. I'm in your Tuesday-Thursday class." She bit her lip. "You spoke to me."

I frowned, not understanding. "You mean what I taught seemed vivid to you? I inspired you to write a better story?"

"Mr. Ingram, no. I mean you *spoke* to me. You stared at me while you were teaching. You ignored the other students. You directed what you said to *me*. When you talked about Hemingway, how Frederic Henry wants to go to bed with Catherine—" She swallowed. "—you were asking me to go to bed with you."

I gaped. To disguise my shock, I quickly lit a cigarette. "You're mistaken."

"But I *heard* you. You kept staring straight at *me*. I felt all the other students knew what you were doing."

"I was only lecturing. I often look at students' faces to make sure they pay attention. You received the wrong impression."

"You weren't asking me to go to bed with you?" Her voice sounded anguished.

"No. I don't trade sex for grades."

"But I don't care about a grade!"

"I'm married. Happily. I've got two children. Anyway, suppose I did intend to proposition you. Would I do it in the middle of a class? I'd be foolish."

"Then you never meant to—" She kept biting her lip.

"I'm sorry."

"But you speak to me! Outside class I hear your voice! When I'm in my room or walking down the street! You talk to me when I'm asleep! You say you want to go to bed with me!"

My skin prickled. I felt frozen. "You're mistaken. Your imagination's playing tricks."

"But I hear your voice so clearly! When I'm studying or—"

"How? If I'm not there."

"You send your thoughts! You concentrate and put your voice inside my mind!"

Adrenaline scalded my stomach. I frantically sought an argument to disillusion her. "Telepathy? I don't believe in it. I've never tried to send my thoughts to you."

"Unconsciously?"

I shook my head from side to side. I couldn't bring myself to tell her: of all the female students in her class, she looked so plain, even if I wasn't married I'd never have wanted sex with her.

"You're studying too hard. You want to do so well you're preoccupied with me. That's why you think you hear my voice when I'm not there. I try to make my lectures vivid. As a consequence, you think I'm speaking totally to you."

"Then you shouldn't teach that way!" she shouted. "It's not fair! It's cruel! It's teasing!" Tears streamed down her face. "You made a fool of me!"

"I didn't mean to."

"But you did! You tricked me! You misled me!"

"No."

She stood so quickly I flinched, afraid she'd lunge at me or scream for help and claim I'd tried to rape her. That damned door. I cursed myself for not insisting she leave it open.

She rushed sobbing toward it. She pawed the knob and stumbled out, hysterically retreating down the stairwell.

Shaken, I stubbed out my cigarette, grabbing another. My chest tightened as I heard the dwindling echo of her wracking sobs, the awkward scuffle of her dimming footsteps, then the low deep rumble of the outside door.

The silence settled over me.

An hour later I found her waiting in class. She'd wiped her tears. The only signs of what had happened were her red and puffy eyes. She sat alertly, pen to paper. I carefully didn't face her as I spoke. She seldom glanced up from her notes.

After class I asked my graduate assistant if he knew her.

"You mean Sam? Sure, I know her. She's been getting Ds. She had a conference with me. Instead of asking how to get a better grade, though, all she did was talk about you, pumping me for information. She's got quite a thing for you. Too bad about her."

"Why?"

"Well, she's so plain, she doesn't have many friends. I doubt she goes out much. There's a problem with her father. She was vague about it, but I had the sense her three sisters are so beautiful that Daddy treats her as the ugly duckling. She wants very much to please him. He ignores her, though. He's practically disowned her. You remind her of him."

"Who? Of her father?"

"She admits you're ten years younger than him, but she says you look exactly like him."

I felt heartsick.

Two days later I found her waiting for me—again at 8 A.M.— outside my office.

Tense, I unlocked the door. As if she heard my thought, she didn't shut it this time. Sitting before my desk, she didn't fidget. She just stared at me.

"It happened again," she said.

"In class I didn't even look at you."

"No, afterward, when I went to the library." She drew an anguished breath. "And later—I ate supper in the dorm. I heard your voice so clearly, I was sure you were in the room."

"What time was that?"

"Five-thirty."

"I was having cocktails with the Dean. Believe me, Sam, I wasn't sending messages to you. I didn't even *think* of you."

"I couldn't have imagined it! You wanted me to go to bed with you!"

"I wanted research money from the Dean. I thought of nothing else. My mind was totally involved in trying to convince him. When I didn't get the money, I was too annoyed to concentrate on anything but getting drunk."

"Your voice—"

"It isn't real. If I sent thoughts to you, wouldn't I admit what I was doing? When you asked me, wouldn't I confirm the message? Why would I deny it?"

"I'm afraid."

"You're troubled by your father."

"What?"

"My graduate assistant says you identify me with your father." She went ashen. "That's supposed to be a secret!"

"Sam, I asked him. He won't lie to me."

"If you remind me of my father, if I want to go to bed with you, then I must want to go to bed with—"

"Sam—"

"—my father! You must think I'm disgusting!"

"No, I think you're confused. You ought to find some help. You ought to see a—"

But she never let me finish. Weeping again, ashamed, hysterical, she bolted from the room.

And that's the last I ever saw of her. An hour later, when I started lecturing, she wasn't in class. A few days later I received a drop-slip from the registrar, informing me she'd canceled all her classes.

I forgot her.

Summer came. Then fall arrived. November. On a rainy Tuesday night, my wife and I stayed up to watch the close results of the election, worried for our presidential candidate.

At 3 A.M. the phone rang. No one calls that late unless . . .

The jangle of the phone made me bang my head as I searched for a beer in the fridge. I rubbed my throbbing skull and swung alarmed as Jean, my wife, came from the living room and squinted toward the kitchen phone.

"It might be just a friend," I said. "Election gossip."

But I worried about our parents. Maybe one of them was sick or . . .

I watched uneasily as Jean picked up the phone.

"Hello?" She listened apprehensively. Frowning, she put her hand across the mouthpiece. "It's for you. A woman."

"What?"

"She's young. She asked for Mr. Ingram."

"Damn, a student."

"At 3 A.M.?"

I almost didn't think to shut the fridge. Annoyed, I yanked the pop-tab off the can of beer. My marriage is successful. I'll admit we've had our troubles. So has every couple. But we've faced those troubles, and we're happy. Jean is thirty-five, attractive, smart, and patient. But her trust in me was clearly tested at that moment. A woman had to know me awfully well to call at 3 A.M.

"Let's find out." I grabbed the phone. To prove my innocence to Jean, I roughly said, "Yeah, what?"

"I heard you." The female voice was frail and plaintive, trembling.

"Who *is* this?" I said angrily.

"It's me."

I heard a low-pitched crackle on the line.

"Who the hell is *me?* Just tell me what your name is."

"Sam."

My knees went weak. I slumped against the wall.

Jean stared. "What's wrong?" Her eyes narrowed with suspicion.

"Sam, it's 3 A.M. What's so damn important you can't wait to call me during office hours?"

"Three? It can't be. No, it's one."

"It's three. For God sake, Sam, I know what time it is."

"Please, don't get angry. On my radio the news announcer said it was one o'clock."

"Where *are* you, Sam?"

"At Berkeley."

"California? Sam, the time-zone difference. In the Midwest it's two hours later. Here it's three o'clock."

". . . I guess I just forgot."

"But that's absurd. Have you been drinking? Are you drunk?"

"No, not exactly."

"What the hell does *that* mean?"

"Well, I took some pills. I'm not sure what they were."

"Oh, Jesus."

"Then I heard you. You were speaking to me."

"No. I told you your mind's playing tricks. The voice isn't real. You're imagining—"

"You called to me. You said you wanted me to go to bed with you. You wanted me to come to you."

"To Iowa? No. You've got to understand. Don't do it. I'm not sending thoughts to you."

"You're lying! Tell me why you're lying!"

"I don't want to go to bed with you. I'm glad you're in Berkeley. Stay there. Get some help. Lord, don't you realize? Those pills. They make you hear my voice. They make you hallucinate."

"I . . ."

"Trust me, Sam. Believe me. I'm not sending thoughts to you. I didn't even know you'd gone to Berkeley. You're two thousand miles away from me. What you're suggesting is impossible."

She didn't answer. All I heard was low-pitched static.

"Sam—"

The dial tone abruptly droned. My stomach sank. Appalled, I kept the phone against my ear. I swallowed dryly, shaking as I set the phone back on its cradle.

Jean glared. "Who was that? She wasn't any 'Sam.' She wants to go to bed with you? At 3 A.M.? What games have you been playing?"

"None." I gulped my beer, but my throat stayed dry. "You'd better sit. I'll get a beer for you."

Jean clutched her stomach.

"It's not what you think. I promise I'm not screwing anybody. But it's bad. I'm scared."

I handed Jean a beer.

"I don't know why it happened. But last spring, at 8 A.M., I went to school and . . ."

Jean listened, troubled. Afterward she asked for Sam's description, somewhat mollified to learn she was plain and pitiful.

"The truth?" Jean asked.

"I promise you."

Jean studied me. "You did nothing to encourage her?"

"I guarantee it. I wasn't aware of her until I found her waiting for me."

"But unconsciously?"

"Sam asked me that as well. I was only lecturing the best way I know how."

Jean kept her eyes on me. She nodded, glancing toward her beer. "Then she's disturbed. There's nothing you can do for her. I'm glad she moved to Berkeley. In your place, I'd have been afraid."

"I *am* afraid. She spooks me."

At a dinner party the next Saturday, I told our host and hostess what had happened, motivated more than just by need to share my fear with someone else, for while the host was both a friend and colleague, he was married to a clinical psychologist. I needed professional advice.

Diane, the hostess, listened with slim interest until halfway through my story, when she suddenly sat straight and peered at me.

I faltered. "What's the matter?"

"Don't stop. What else?"

I frowned and finished, waiting for Diane's reaction. Instead she poured more wine. She offered more lasagna.

"Something bothered you."

She tucked her long black hair behind her ears. "It could be nothing."

"I need to know."

She nodded grimly. "I can't make a diagnosis merely on the basis of your story. I'd be irresponsible."

"But hypothetically . . ."

"And *only* hypothetically. She hears your voice. That's symptomatic of a severe disturbance. Paranoia, for example. Schizophrenia. The man who shot John Lennon heard a voice. And so did Manson. So did Son of Sam."

"My God," Jean said. "Her name." She set her fork down loudly.

"The parallel occurred to me," Diane said. "Chuck, if she identifies you with her father, she might be dangerous to Jean and to the children."

"Why?"

"Jealousy. To hurt the equivalent of her mother and her rival sisters."

I felt sick; the wine turned sour in my stomach.

"There's another possibility. No more encouraging. If you continue to reject her, she could be dangerous to you. Instead of dealing with her father, she might redirect her rage and jealousy toward you. By killing you, she'd be venting her frustration toward her father."

I felt panicked. "For the *good* news."

"Understand, I'm speaking hypothetically. Possibly she's lying to you, and she doesn't hear your voice. Or, as you guessed, the drugs she takes might make her hallucinate. There could be many explanations. Without seeing her, without the proper tests, I wouldn't dare to judge her symptoms. You're a friend, so I'm compromising. Possibly she's homicidal."

"Tell me what to do."

"For openers, I'd stay away from her."

"I'm *trying*. She called from California. She's threatening to come back here to see me."

"Talk her out of it."

"I'm no psychologist. I don't know what to say to her."

"Suggest she get professional advice."

"I tried that."

"Try again. But if you find her at your office, don't go in the room with her. Find other people. Crowds protect you."

"But at 8 A.M. there's no one in the building."

"Think of some excuse to leave her. Jean, if she comes to the house, don't let her in."

Jean paled. "I've never seen her. How could I identify her?"

"Chuck described her. Don't take chances. Don't trust anyone who might resemble her, and keep a close watch on the children."

"*How?* Rebecca's twelve. Sue's nine. I can't insist they stay around the house."

Diane turned her wine glass, saying nothing.

". . . Oh, dear Lord," Jean said.

The next few weeks were hellish. Every time the phone rang, Jean and I jerked, startled, staring at it. But the calls were from our friends or from our children's friends or from some insulation/magazine/home-siding salesman. Every day I mustered courage as I climbed the stairwell to my office. Silent prayers were answered. Sam was never there. My tension dissipated. I began to feel she no longer was obsessed with me.

Thanksgiving came—the last day of peace I've known. We went to church. Our parents live too far away for us to share the feast with them. But we invited friends to dinner. We watched football. I helped Jean make the dressing for the turkey. I made both the pumpkin pies. The friends we'd invited were my colleague and his wife, the clinical psychologist. She asked if my student had continued to harass me. Shaking my head from side to side, I grinned and raised my glass in special thanks.

The guests stayed late to watch a movie with us. Jean and I felt pleasantly exhausted, mellowed by good food, good drink, good friends, when after midnight we washed all the dishes, went to bed, made love, and drifted wearily to sleep.

The phone rang, shocking me awake. I fumbled toward the bedside lamp. Jean's eyes went wide with fright. She clutched my arm and pointed toward the clock. It was 3 A.M.

The phone kept ringing.

"Don't," Jean said.

"Suppose it's someone else."

"You know it isn't."

"If it's Sam and I don't answer, she might come to the house instead of phoning."

"For God's sake, make her stop."

I grabbed the phone, but my throat wouldn't work.

"I'm coming to you," the voice wailed.

"Sam?"

"I heard you. I won't disappoint you. I'll be there soon."

"No. Wait. Listen."

"I've been listening. I hear you all the time. The anguish in your voice. You're begging me to come to you, to hold you, to make love to you."

"That isn't true."

"You say your wife's jealous of me. I'll convince her she isn't being fair. I'll make her let you go. Then we'll be happy."

"Sam, where are you? Still in Berkeley?"

"Yes. I spent Thanksgiving by myself. My father didn't want me to come home."

"You have to stay there, Sam. I didn't send my voice. You need advice. You need to see a doctor. Will you do that for me? As a favor?"

"I already did. But Dr. Campbell doesn't understand. He thinks I'm imagining what I hear. He humors me. He doesn't realize how much you love me."

"Sam, you have to talk to him again. You have to tell him what you plan to do."

"I can't wait any longer. I'll be there soon. I'll be with you."

My heart pounded frantically. I heard a roar in my head. I flinched as the phone was yanked away from me.

Jean shouted to the mouthpiece, "Stay away from us! Don't call again! Stop terrorizing—"

Jean stared wildly at me. "No one's there. The line went dead. I hear just the dial tone."

I'm writing this as quickly as I can. I don't have much more time. It's almost three o'clock.

That night, we didn't try to go back to sleep. We couldn't. We got dressed and went downstairs where, drinking coffee, we decided what to do. At eight, as soon as we'd sent the kids to school, we drove to the police.

They listened sympathetically, but there was no way they could help us. After all, Sam hadn't broken any law. Her calls weren't obscene; it was difficult to prove harassment; she'd made no overt threats. Unless she harmed us, there was nothing the police could do.

"Protect us," I insisted.

"How?" the sergeant said.

"Assign an officer to guard the house."

"How long? A day, a week, a month? That woman might not even bother you again. We're overworked and understaffed. I'm sorry—I can't spare an officer whose only duty is to watch you. I can send a car to check the house from time to time. No more than that. But if this woman does show up and bother you, then call us. We'll take care of her."

"But that might be too late."

We took the children home from school. Sam couldn't have arrived from California yet, but what else could we do? I don't own any guns. If all of us stayed together, we had some chance for protection.

That was Friday. I slept lightly. Three A.M., the phone rang. It was Sam, of course.

"I'm coming."

"Sam, where are you?"

"Reno."

"You're not flying."

"No, I can't."

"Turn back, Sam. Go to Berkeley. See that doctor."

"I can't wait to see you."

"Please—"

The dial tone was droning.

I phoned Berkeley information. Sam had mentioned Dr. Campbell. But the operator couldn't find him in the yellow pages.

"Try the University," I blurted. "Student Counseling."

I was right. A Dr. Campbell was a university psychiatrist. On Saturday I couldn't reach him at his office, but a woman answered at his home. He wouldn't be available until the afternoon. At four o'clock I finally got through to him.

"You've got a patient named Samantha Perry," I began.

"I did. Not anymore."

"I know. She's left for Iowa. She wants to see me. I'm afraid. I think she might be dangerous."

"Well, you don't have to worry."

"She's not dangerous?"

"Potentially she was."

"But tell me what to do when she arrives. You're treating her. You'll know what I should do."

"No, Mr. Ingram, she won't come to see you. On Thanksgiving night, at 1 A.M., she killed herself. An overdose of drugs."

My vision failed. I clutched the kitchen table to prevent myself from falling. "That's impossible."

"I saw the body. I identified it."

"But she called that night."

"What time?"

"At 3 A.M. Midwestern time."

"Or one o'clock in California. No doubt after or before she took the drugs. She didn't leave a note, but she called you."

"She gave no indication—"

"She mentioned you quite often. She was morbidly attracted to you. She had an extreme, unhealthy certainty that she was telepathic, that you put your voice inside her mind."

"I know that! Was she paranoid or homicidal?"

"Mr. Ingram, I've already said too much. Although she's dead, I can't violate her confidence."

"But I don't think she's dead."

"I beg your pardon?"

"If she died on Thursday night, then tell me how she called again on *Friday* night."

The line hummed. I sensed the doctor's hesitation. "Mr. Ingram, you're upset. You don't know what you're saying. You've confused the nights."

"I'm telling you she called again on Friday!"

"And I'm telling you she died on *Thursday*. Either someone's tricking you, or else . . ." The doctor swallowed with discomfort.

"Or?" I trembled. "*I'm* the one who's hearing voices?"

"Mr. Ingram, don't upset yourself. You're honestly confused."

I slowly put the phone down, terrified. "I'm sure I heard her voice."

That night, Sam called again. At 3 A.M. From Salt Lake City. When I handed Jean the phone, she heard just the dial tone.

"But you know the goddamn phone rang!" I insisted.

"Maybe a short circuit. Chuck, I'm telling you there was no one on the line."

Then Sunday. Three A.M. Cheyenne, Wyoming. Coming closer.

But she couldn't be if she was dead.

The student paper at the University subscribes to all the other major student papers. Monday, Jean and I left the children with friends and drove to its office. Friday's copy of the Berkeley campus paper had arrived. In desperation I searched its pages. "There!" A two-inch item. Sudden student death. Samantha Perry. Tactfully, no cause was given.

Outside in the parking lot, Jean said, "Now do you believe she's dead?"

"Then tell me why I hear her voice! I've got to be crazy if I think I hear a corpse!"

"You're feeling guilty that she killed herself because of you. You shouldn't. There was nothing you could do to stop her. You've been losing too much sleep. Your imagination's taking over."

"You admit you heard the phone ring!"

"Yes, it's true. I can't explain that. If the phone's broken, we'll have it fixed. To put your mind at rest, we'll get a new, unlisted number."

I felt better. After several drinks, I even got some sleep.

But Monday night, again the phone rang. Three A.M. I jerked awake. Cringing, I insisted Jean answer it. But she heard just the dial tone. I grabbed the phone. Of course, I heard Sam's voice.

"I'm almost there. I'll hurry. I'm in Omaha."

"This number isn't listed!"

"But you told me the new one. Your wife's the one who changed it. She's trying to keep us apart. I'll make her sorry. Darling, I can't wait to be with you."

I screamed. Jean jerked away from me.

"Sam, you've got to stop! I spoke to Dr. Campbell!"

"No. He wouldn't dare. He wouldn't violate my trust."

"He said you were dead!"

"I couldn't live without you. Soon we'll be together."

Shrieking, I woke the children, so hysterical Jean had to call an ambulance. Two interns struggled to sedate me.

Omaha was one day's drive from where we live. Jean came to visit me in the hospital on Tuesday.

"Are you feeling better?" Jean frowned, troubled.

"Please, you have to humor me," I said. "All right? Suspect I've gone crazy, but for God sake, humor me. I can't prove what I'm thinking, but I know you're in danger. I am too. You have to get the children and leave town. You have to hide somewhere. Tonight at 3 A.M. she'll reach the house."

Jean stared with pity.

"Promise me!" I said.

She saw the anguish on my face and nodded.

"Maybe she won't try the house," I said. "She might come here. I have to get away. I'm not sure how, but later, when you're gone, I'll find a way to leave."

Jean peered at me, distressed; her voice sounded totally discouraged. "Chuck."

"I'll check the house when I get out of here. If you're still there, you know you'll make me more upset."

"I promise. I'll take Susan and Rebecca, and we'll drive somewhere."

"I love you."

Jean began to cry. "I won't know where you are."

"If I survive this, I'll get word to you."

"But how?"

"The English department. I'll leave a message with the secretary."

Jean leaned down to kiss me, crying, certain I'd lost my mind.

I reached the house that night. As she'd promised, Jean had left
with the children. I got in my sports car and raced to the Inter-
state.

A Chicago hotel where at 3 A.M. Sam called from Iowa. She'd
heard my voice. She said I'd told her where I was, but she was
hurt and angry. "Tell me why you're running."

I fled from Chicago in the middle of the night, driving until I
absolutely had to rest. I checked in here at 1 A.M. In Johnstown,
Pennsylvania. I can't sleep. I've got an awful feeling. Last night
Sam repeated, "Soon you'll join me." In the desk I found this
stationery.

God, it's 3 A.M. I pray I'll see the sun come up.

It's almost four. She didn't phone. I can't believe I escaped, but
I keep staring at the phone.

It's four. Dear Christ, I hear the ringing.

Finally I've realized. Sam killed herself at one. In Iowa the
time-zone difference made it three. But I'm in Pennsylvania. In
the East. A different time zone. One o'clock in California would
be *four* o'clock, not three, in Pennsylvania.

Now.

The ringing persists. But I've realized something else. This
hotel's unusual, designed to seem like a home.

The ringing?

God help me, it's the doorbell.